*If Jace offered her just a crumb of warmth, Danielle knew sh̶ ̶ ̶ ̶ ̶ in love with ̶ ̶ ̶*

She remembered the ̶ ̶ ̶ house, snuggled in his ̶ ̶ ̶ wrapped in Jace's arm ̶ ̶ ̶

Warm, protected, cared ̶ ̶. All hers simply for the asking when Jace had wanted her.

It was over. All of it. She needed to hang on to that. Love wasn't possible between her and Jace, at least not mutual love. She needed to remember the purpose of her marriage to him. It was little more than a business arrangement and she needed to keep her distance.

If only Jace would agree....

Dear Reader,

Silhouette Romance novels aren't just for other women—the wonder of a Silhouette Romance is that it can touch *your* heart. And this month's selections are guaranteed to leave you smiling!

In Suzanne McMinn's engaging BUNDLES OF JOY title, *The Billionaire and the Bassinet,* a blue blood finds his hardened heart irrevocably tamed. This month's FABULOUS FATHERS offering by Jodi O'Donnell features an emotional, heartwarming twist you won't soon forget; in *Dr. Dad to the Rescue,* a man discovers strength and the healing power of love from one *very* special lady. *Marrying O'Malley,* the renegade who'd been her childhood nemesis, seemed the perfect way for a bride-to-be to thwart an unwanted betrothal—until their unlikely alliance stirred an even more incredible passion; don't miss this latest winner by Elizabeth August!

*The Cowboy Proposes...Marriage?* Get the charming lowdown as WRANGLERS & LACE continues with this sizzling story by Cathy Forsythe. Cara Colter will make you laugh and cry with *A Bride Worth Waiting For,* the story of the boy next door who *didn't* get the girl, but who'll stop at nothing to have her now. For readers who love powerful, dramatic stories, you won't want to miss *Paternity Lessons,* Maris Soule's uplifting FAMILY MATTERS tale.

Enjoy this month's titles—and please drop me a line about *why* you keep coming back to Romance. I want to make sure we continue fulfilling *your* dreams!

Regards,

*Mary-Theresa Hussey*

Mary-Theresa Hussey
Senior Editor Silhouette Romance

Please address questions and book requests to:
Silhouette Reader Service
U.S.: 3010 Walden Ave., P.O. Box 1325, Buffalo, NY 14269
Canadian: P.O. Box 609, Fort Erie, Ont. L2A 5X3

# THE COWBOY PROPOSES...MARRIAGE?

## Cathy Forsythe

*Silhouette*

R O M A N C E™

Published by Silhouette Books

**America's Publisher of Contemporary Romance**

To Jerimiah and Brandon
Both heroes in their own special way
I'm proud to call you my sons

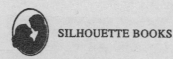

SILHOUETTE BOOKS

ISBN 0-373-19387-4

THE COWBOY PROPOSES...MARRIAGE?

Copyright © 1999 by Cathy Forsythe

Visit us at www.romance.net

Printed in U.S.A.

**Books by Cathy Forsythe**

Silhouette Romance

*The Marriage Contract* #1167
*The Cowboy Proposes...Marriage?* #1387

## CATHY FORSYTHE

After dealing with the mountains of mud and a zoo full of pets generated by two growing boys. Cathy is ready to settle down to the much cleaner job of writing. With the continued support of her husband, who is hero material himself, she is constantly searching for interesting characters and new story ideas. Now, if she can just convince her dog not to be jealous of the computer....

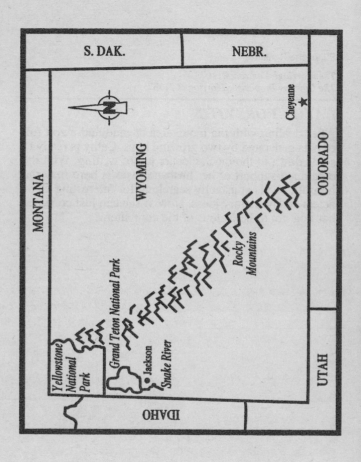

# Chapter One

"I have an idea of the style I want for my wedding gown, but I haven't…"

A flash of gray distracted Danielle Simmons from the flow of conversation, but when she turned, it was gone. And suddenly she lost interest in the chatter about her upcoming wedding.

Restless, edgy, she excused herself, hoping to locate the source of the unease prickling her spine. Studying the room carefully, she slowly circled the guests.

Everything was perfect. The food was plentiful and artfully prepared by the caterers, the champagne expensive and abundant, the guests cleverly blended.

She hoped.

The flash of gray appeared in her vision again, but before she could look, Raymond took her arm. "Having fun, darling?"

His touch was gentle, a soft stroke on her arm

that should have sent tingles racing across her skin. But it didn't.

Not the way another man's touch had, once upon a time.

In spite of the niggling doubts tormenting her, Danielle forced a smile to her carefully painted lips. "Of course. Who wouldn't with a room full of our nearest and dearest friends?" Half of whom she couldn't remember the names of.

He nuzzled her ear and she leaned closer to him. And waited. In vain. There was no rush of desire, no flare of warmth. Only a deep affection, a friendly attachment, for the man she was engaged to. Maybe if she'd never experienced the surge of passion, she wouldn't be disappointed every time Raymond touched her. But she *had* reveled in her own sexuality—had even involved her heart in the dangerous game of love.

Only to have it thrown back in her face.

Raymond gently pressed his lips to her cheek, his breath brushing her skin as he spoke. "We'll share a dance at the stroke of midnight—after your father makes a toast to our engagement. Then we'll run off these freeloaders and have some fun."

Danielle smiled, certain she was feeling the first twinges of a headache. And just as certain that Raymond would be kind and understanding when she sent him home early.

From behind them, a husky voice interrupted, a voice coated with sarcasm. "Isn't that sweet?"

The rich baritone slid over her, dancing a kaleidoscope of images across Danielle's thoughts. Tall. Broad shoulders. A dark-haired man, cowboy hat set at a cocky angle, blue eyes sparkling with a devilish gleam, teasing, laughing—loving.

It had been eleven years since she'd last heard that voice—an eternity—but certainly not long enough.

She turned, mouth dry. He stood, detached from the crowd, out of place in this gathering of sequined formals and black tuxedos. The passing years were etched on his face, but the rugged lines only added to his allure.

Danielle blinked, almost scrubbed at her carefully made-up eyes, but he didn't disappear.

It couldn't be. He wouldn't dare. She wouldn't let him.

Forcing herself to move, she took a step forward, her lungs beginning to ache from lack of air. She tried to ignore the pain biting into her soul when she looked at him. After all these years, she should be over him.

"I understand congratulations are in order. Let me be the first." The man leisurely reached out and grasped her fluted glass, taking it from her and raising it in a toast. "To the loving couple." He nodded to Raymond.

Then the cowboy turned to Danielle. She felt trapped in the blue ice of his eyes—eyes speaking of all the memories that stood between them. Her own anger warred with the dregs of pain she harbored from their shared past.

"And here's to you, darlin'." He tipped back the glass and drained the fine champagne as if it were water. One dark eyebrow lifted as he thunked the delicate crystal on a nearby table. "A little dry for my taste, but not bad for the exorbitant price I'm sure you paid.''

His eyes challenged her to do something. About him. About his presence at her engagement party. And she'd never been able to resist a challenge.

Especially when Jace Farrell issued it.

Her back teeth snapped together, but Danielle managed to paste a smile onto her face. ''Jace, how good of you to stop by.'' The polite words almost choked her as she turned to Raymond, hoping her smile hadn't become a snarl. ''Sweetheart, I'll be right back. I need to speak with an old friend,'' she said.

Raymond frowned and tightened his hold on her for a brief second. Gently pulling away from him, she walked toward Jace, disconcerted by the discovery that the powerful magnetism between them remained so strong. Not even time and sorrow had managed to fade their attraction.

Danielle grabbed his elbow and tried to urge him toward the patio, but he just stood there—a sardonic grin twisting his lips—and watched her.

''I'd like to talk with you, Jace. Privately. Won't you join me outside?'' The heat from his skin burned through his clothes, singeing her fingers, but she couldn't pull away. With Jace she had always felt that rush of awareness she'd been looking for. But he had almost destroyed her once, had trampled her heart and her love. She refused to give him that chance again.

''Only if you say please,'' he murmured, the words for her ears only. ''Pretty please.''

The deep tone of his voice stroked her and she clenched her teeth tighter to suppress her trembling reaction. He'd used her attraction to control her emotions in the past. She wasn't about to allow it to happen again. No matter how much it hurt.

"Pretty please, Jace?" Danielle asked, amazed the words sounded so clear through clenched teeth.

Pulling her hand through the crook of his arm, he laid his fingers across hers, effectively holding her captive. Without another word, he started for the double French doors on the other side of the room.

The past was repeating itself. The first time she met Jace, he'd stood with her on the same deck. But that time, her rose-colored glasses had been firmly in place. Time and betrayal had changed that, had changed her.

The Wyoming night was cool, a welcome relief to her burning face and bare shoulders. Jace had always managed to raise her temperature, either with anger or with passion. But she'd never been complacent around him—had never been the way she was with Raymond.

Danielle tugged at her hand, needing some distance, but Jace refused to let her go. They walked in silence toward the darkened edge of the porch, the soft glow of the interior lights allowing her to see more than she wanted.

She fingered the gold locket at her throat, drawing strength from its familiar presence, strength she suspected she would need to get through these next few minutes.

When she couldn't stand the escalating tension another second, she stopped, and Jace finally released her but didn't step away. Grabbing the wooden railing, she braced herself, needing moral as well as physical support.

"What are you doing here?" She didn't turn to him when she made her demand, instead she stared into the endless darkness broken only by a scattering of stars in the Wyoming sky, remembering happier times, times when she thought she'd spend the rest of her life in this man's arms.

She ached for the future that had never happened.

And his lack of response proved he could still manage to irritate her by doing absolutely nothing.

"Damn it, Jace." She spun, determined to face him when she unleashed her anger. "I asked you—"

His mouth swooped down on hers without warning, without hesitation. Danielle sucked in a breath of surprise, realizing her error when the unmistakable scent of Jace filled her head—a scent that was all natural, all man, and only Jace.

Even that thought melted away as his lips seared her mouth. Without a hint of gentle persuasion, he urged her lips apart. When she resisted, he reached up with his free hand and tugged at her chin with his thumb. The invasion of his tongue was a bitterly welcomed onslaught, one she unconsciously savored as she became reacquainted with his taste.

More memories crashed back, breaking through the door she'd spent years building to suppress them. The loving, the laughing...the fighting. They'd never been able to agree on anything except the fact they'd desired each other. Finally, even that had fallen apart and Danielle had done the only thing possible.

She'd walked away.

And regretted the loss every day since.

But she couldn't forgive his deception, his lies. Couldn't forgive the fact that he hadn't loved her enough.

She moaned deep in her throat as Jace began to stroke her neck. Imprisoning her chin with his long fingers, he broke away, leaving a whisper of air between them.

He stared at her, and even in the semidarkness, she sensed the fire now burning in his eyes. She'd always had the power to put it there, always reveled in her ability to drive a small wedge in his ironclad control.

But it had never been enough. She'd wanted more from him. She'd wanted all of him. And he'd never relinquished the reins he held on his emotions.

Even though he couldn't give her the words she'd so desperately needed to hear, she'd been willing to stay, to keep trying, to love him. Because what they had shared was special, something she hadn't wanted to give up. Then he'd turned away, trading her love for a much more seductive mistress...a mistress she couldn't compete with because it wasn't even another woman.

Her memories fragmented when Jace leaned back against the railing, planting his legs apart and pulling her against him. The remembered sensation of his hard-muscled thighs burned through her clothing.

"No, Jace." Her whisper made barely a sound, but she knew he'd heard her.

"Yes, Dani."

He pressed his lips to hers and her small token

of resistance faded away along with the years that had separated them. Heaven help her, she needed this man.

Tipping her chin back, he left a blazing trail of sensation down the side of her neck. His lips sought and received a response from her sensitive skin, a response no other man had ever ignited. Heat shivered over her, leaving her weak.

When he brushed her hair aside to nip at her shoulder, she knew she had to stop this madness...before her fiancé found her here, with another man, doing something that shattered her very soul.

"Jace, please."

He paused in his explorations and she let out the breath that clogged her lungs, harboring a faint hope that for once he might understand and leave her a small measure of peace. But Jace had never been understanding.

"Please, what?" He smoothed away the hair that had fallen across her eyes. "Please kiss me? Please carry me away? Please make love to me?"

If only it could be that easy for them. Struggling simply to draw an even breath, she couldn't break through the sensations bombarding her to formulate a response.

"Is your fiancé willing to share, then?"

Her protest became tangled with her conflicting feelings, making it impossible to give him the blistering response he deserved.

When she didn't answer, he grinned, but sarcasm dripped from his words. "He wouldn't mind if he came out here right now, is that it? Poor Dani." He shook his head, managing to pull her closer, close enough that she had no doubt just how aroused he was.

"Jace, stop." She pushed against his chest, needing to escape, to regain her equilibrium. "He would mind, very much. And so do I." The lie tasted bitter, but she knew she had to say it.

"You don't feel like you mind." Jace cocked his head to study her. "You don't kiss like you mind. Another lie, Dani?"

"My name is Danielle."

"To all these high-society fluff balls, maybe. To me, you'll always be my Dani girl."

"I'm not your girl anymore, Jace. I haven't been for years." She pushed away from him again.

Somehow, he managed to use her efforts against her and wedge her tighter between his legs. Danielle's cheeks burned and she was thankful for the shadows. There had been a time when she'd relished this position, had loved to play the sexy tease for Jace, couldn't resist every opportunity to turn him on.

That was over now.

"So *Daddy* has picked out the perfect man this time."

Jace traced her lips with his finger, the work-roughened skin stoking her senses even further.

"I'll bet Raymond has lots of money to share. And what does he get in return?"

She didn't answer, couldn't answer, against the ache swelling through her. All she wanted was to be loved, to be cherished for herself and not what she could bring a man. And that had become the impossible dream for her. Instead, she'd become a pawn in a business world she was learning to hate.

"Ah." Jace took her chin in his hand, forcing her to look at him. "Raymond gets you, doesn't he? A prize society catch. A woman with connections, looks and all the training an important man needs."

The ache turned into a piercing shaft of pain. She'd hoped Raymond loved her a little bit, but she feared Jace was right. Danielle Simmons was trained to be the perfect wife, and in her father's circle, that was a commodity to be traded for high stakes.

Jace tugged her a little closer as if knowing he'd lost her attention, and she couldn't stop the heat from rising in her cheeks.

"You never used to blush when you were in my arms."

"I never used to object to being in your arms, either. It's over, Jace. So why are you here?"

"I'm here because you're mine. And *I* have no intention of sharing you...with Raymond or anyone else."

She made a fist and pounded it into his chest once. Then she raised her left hand and waved it in his face, desperate to make him understand, to make him go away. "In case you hadn't noticed, I'm engaged. To another man, Jace. This ring makes me his, not yours."

He grabbed her wrist and held her hand immobile. She tried to twist away, afraid of the sudden anger that flared in his eyes. Jace Farrell was capable of anything to get what he wanted and she wouldn't be surprised if he tore the ring from her finger and threw the glittering diamond over the ledge.

"Nice rock." A smile that held no humor twisted his lips. "But I can do better than that. How about it, Dani? If I buy you a bigger ring than his, will you marry me?"

For a brief flash of time, she dared to hope that he really meant it, that their shattered love could become a reality. But that dream was quickly dashed when she saw the anger in his eyes.

The bitterness in his tone made her feel a twinge of guilt. Dragging at her hand, she only succeeded in hurting herself. "Jace, stop. This isn't a game."

She hadn't ever asked much of Jace. Never anything more than she was willing to return. Never more than the truth. Never more than his love. Even now, she longed to hear him say the words. But as usual, he talked about wants and needs, not of love. She hardened herself against his pain.

It was the only way she could save herself.

"You traded my love for money. I can't—won't—ever forgive that. What we had is over. Maybe you can settle down with one of those little ranch girls, one who wants to live in the middle of nowhere with a herd of cows and a million tumbleweeds."

"Don't exaggerate, darlin'. Last time you were out at the ranch, there couldn't have been more than ten thousand tumbleweeds. And most of those blew away before you left."

The anger washed over her, eroding her control. She balled her hand into a fist and struck out at him again. But Jace seemed to barely exert himself before he had her fist cradled in the palm of his hand.

Closing his fingers around hers, he gently pushed her arm away, twisting her hand behind her back.

Then he guided her other hand down to join the first. Wrapping both her wrists in his long fingers, he brought his free hand up to stroke her neck.

She tried to pull away, knowing his touch was like spontaneous combustion to her body, but he held her trapped. Her lips tightened with anger, but she choked back the words. Any reaction would only encourage him.

Jace traced her collarbone with his finger before moving downward to follow the neckline of her dress—the dress Raymond had picked out for her with a slight leer, saying he would enjoy exploring the possibilities revealed later. The dress that was all red, shimmering satin and clinging lace.

Jace's finger slipped inside the neckline, dipping just a fraction lower to explore her heated skin. She tried to suppress the shiver that rippled through her—tried and failed.

Jace smiled, his mouth tight with contained anger, and explored farther.

"This doesn't prove anything." She bit her lip when she realized her voice was a breathless whisper that contradicted her words.

"You're mine, Dani. You'll always be mine and we both know it." He stroked a path to the top of her other breast.

"What we had was over far too long ago to even discuss it."

"It was never over. I just needed some time to put my life back together. Now I expect you to honor your promise to marry me."

"No, Jace." Her breathing had quickened, making it difficult to infuse her voice with anger. When she pulled against the hand that held her, he didn't relent.

His finger dropped lower, skimming down her breast, making tantalizing circles, each one edging closer to the sensitive nub. Her nipples tightened in anticipation, but he paused, didn't pursue his explorations, didn't offer her any relief.

"You're going to marry me, Dani girl. No one else."

He'd done it—thrown down the gauntlet—challenged her to prove him wrong. And she was just the woman to do it. Outrage broke through the desire shadowing her mind. Danielle lifted her foot, intending to bring her heel down on his instep. Even through his boots, it was bound to get his attention.

Effortlessly, Jace dropped his hand to her leg and cupped her thigh, suspending her foot in the air. Her narrow skirt inched up, revealing much more skin than she wanted. He took full advantage of the show, dropping his gaze to watch as the dress crept even farther toward indecency.

He tugged her leg higher, wedging her more tightly against him at the same time. Brushing his lips against hers, he smiled. "I know you're anxious to get closer, but do you think this is the right place?"

Rage boiled through her, but she was helpless to do anything about it. It was all she could do to balance on one three-inch heel since he still held her hands behind her back.

"Damn it, Jace." Her soft curse carried all the hurt, all the agony, of the past. "I've finally found the life I was raised to live and I refuse to let you ruin it. Go away.''

Silence pulsed between them. Finally, Jace let her foot drop back to the floor. But he did it ever so slowly, letting his touch caress the silk stockings covering her thigh. Her skin felt a rush of cool air as he released her hands, then grasped her shoulders and moved her away from him.

''You will marry me. And this time, you need me. Your daddy needs me.'' His smile held little humor. ''I'll save you both. Just say the word.'' His voice dropped to a low threat. ''Wooing a woman is like taming a filly. A man needs time and patience to get exactly what he wants.''

He stroked his callused fingers across her cheek, causing remembered sensations to ripple through her.

''And I want you. I've run out of time.'' His lips twisted as the silence stretched between them. ''Ran out of patience long ago. So now we play the game my way.''

He paused as if waiting for her response, but she was too shocked to give him one.

''Twenty-four hours.'' He glanced at his watch, marking the time. ''I'll be waiting to hear from you. And I'll expect your answer to be yes. Don't forget, *Danielle*, I have my own money this time. Enough to buy and sell your father. Enough to bail out your little family business. And wouldn't you rather marry the devil you know?''

A tangled combination of desire and fear knotted her stomach. His words held the quality of a threat. Was he capable of destroying her father if he didn't get what he wanted?

Without warning, he reached for her again. Molding her body against his, he kissed her, all his demands reflected in his lips. He wanted her complete surrender, her total capitulation—and would settle for nothing less.

For one insane flicker of time, she actually considered giving in to him.

"What the hell is going on out here?"

Raymond's voice slowly penetrated the sensual fog clouding her thoughts. Danielle tried to pull away, but Jace only pulled her closer, if that was possible. Finally, she wrenched her mouth from his and gasped for air.

Raymond reached for her, his touch far from gentle when he grabbed her shoulder. "Danielle, what do you think you're doing?"

Jace stiffened, then pushed his way between her and Raymond. Danielle knew there was trouble brewing, knew she needed to put a stop to Jace. But she didn't know how.

"Get out of my way, cowboy. Danielle has some explaining to do. And she'd better do it quickly."

Raymond tried to shoulder Jace aside, but Jace simply stepped in his path. Jace's voice was hard, a threat in itself. "Don't talk to my future wife that way."

Danielle stood by helplessly as her plans crumbled at her feet. There was little sense in trying to explain. She could see by Raymond's expression that he wouldn't listen, wouldn't believe her. She was about to lose it all and didn't have a clue how to stop the disaster.

"I think you have the facts all wrong, cowboy." Raymond tried to push Jace aside again, but Jace didn't even bother moving this time; he just stood solid.

"*Your* engagement is off, pretty boy. Get over it and get out."

Raymond glared at Jace, then narrowed his eyes at her. "You're making a huge mistake, Danielle." His movements deliberate, Raymond pulled a check from his pocket, the check that represented the salvation of her father's business. "I guess you won't need this after all."

Panic threatened to steal her voice. "Raymond..."

He shook his head. "You can't explain what I just witnessed with pretty words, Danielle. Don't even try."

Danielle stepped forward, knowing she had to stop him, but Jace blocked her way. One hand outstretched helplessly, she watched as Raymond tore the check into small pieces. With an angry flourish, he let the scraps flutter to the ground. As her future floated away on a cool breeze, Raymond stalked back into the house.

She wanted to call him back, to explain, but what words would be strong enough, convincing enough? What words would she be able to force past the fear clogging her throat?

Jace observed it all, then turned to study Danielle, his gaze sliding over her with an intense possessiveness. He touched one finger to his hat in salute, then simply walked inside. His boots sounded on the floor, a death knell to Danielle's only chance at helping her father.

Her body seemed frozen, her thoughts immobile as her gaze was drawn to the bright lights glaring through the French doors. Everyone had stopped and was staring at the stage where the orchestra had just finished a song. With a cold shiver that had little to do with the temperature, Danielle realized it was exactly midnight. She watched as Raymond said something to her father, then left without a backward glance.

Danielle forced herself to move forward, but one step inside the doorway, she froze. Her father had seen her and the look in his eyes halted her heartbeat.

She had failed.

She had failed him and the family fortune and that was unforgivable.

She pulled her lip between her teeth as she spotted Jace disappearing through the doorway. He'd mentioned nothing of love—only money. So far, money had only made her life miserable. Why couldn't anyone just love her for herself?

This engagement to Raymond was the same way things had been done in her family for years. Her mother had married for business reasons and so had Danielle's grandmother. Danielle had been certain she would, too.

If only Jace hadn't captured her heart so completely.

If only he didn't tempt her so thoroughly.

If only he hadn't hurt her so badly.

If only...

Danielle hung her head, letting one tear escape before she regained her control. After taking a moment to collect her thoughts, she carefully wiped away any trace of her emotions and squared her shoulders, determined to return to the party and be the perfect hostess.

But her father was making a terse announcement that due to an unexpected emergency, the party was ending early. Then he stepped off the stage and motioned for Danielle to follow him.

And she knew with dreaded certainty that her difficulties were only beginning.

# Chapter Two

She was late.

Jace jerked back the sleeve of his shirt and glared at his watch. Thirty-three minutes late.

He knew about Simmons's bank note. Knew it was due in less than one week—that Danielle's father didn't have the reserves to pay the million dollar debt. And Jace knew Danielle was willing to sacrifice herself to save her father.

Jace had backed her into an impossible corner and still she dared defy him. Jace shared a grim smile with the dark night. Danielle had always stood up to him, had been one of the rare people who challenged him even when rage boiled through him. He admired her grit. But even that wasn't going to save her this time. She would marry him. Or suffer the consequences.

He gazed out at the black shadows covering the wide expanse of Wyoming range. He was the second generation of Farrells to work this land, had been raised here and now devoted his life to the ranch. He'd made his holdings grow and flourish in spite of the odds.

And he wasn't ashamed to admit he loved every acre.

The mountains graced the sky in the distance, the rugged Teton Range as unforgiving as the weather. When his father died, he'd left behind an almost worthless patch of dried sagebrush. But Jace had been young, full of fire, full of determination. He knew what he wanted and had been determined to get it.

Then he'd met Danielle Simmons.

Suddenly, he'd wanted more. He'd dared to think he could have it all. He wanted someone to share his life with, to celebrate the good and help shoulder the bad. But he should have known better, should have realized that life just wasn't that simple.

The year he'd met Danielle had been the end of his first year on his own. The harsh winter had cost him more of his herd than he could afford and prices had crashed to rock bottom. He'd been short on cash to begin with but stood to lose it all if he didn't do something. And he'd needed to do something fast, so he'd looked for a loan.

But the banks were afraid to give money to another troubled rancher. Jace had been forced to seek out private investors. Danielle's father had expressed interest and Jace had thought his troubles were over.

It was then that he learned the bitter lesson that no matter how hard he worked, how big he dreamed, he'd never be good enough for the social elite who had homes in the Jackson Hole area. He would always soil his hands on a regular basis and drive a truck that was layered with dirt because it was used for real work.

Memories of Danielle drifted through his thoughts. Last night, she had been different. She had been a woman instead of the girl he'd fallen for so long ago—the girl who had shredded his heart and his self-respect. The girl who had almost destroyed him and his dreams.

Danielle, the woman, tantalized in new and exciting ways. He could, would make love to her again. The excitement was still there. But she wouldn't touch his heart. Never again would he open himself to the pain of such a betrayal.

Jace glanced at his watch and anticipation curled through him. Soon. She'd be here soon. Danielle couldn't refuse him. He'd forced a change in her life, had made her face the reality of what she was doing and acknowledge that life with Raymond would be far from perfect. Jace had seen it all in her eyes last night.

And he'd made her want. Him.

Almost as badly as he wanted her. When he'd held her, he'd felt her longing in the trembling that shuddered through her, sensed it in the heat of her mouth.

Jace sucked in a breath, trying to calm his raging libido.

The glow of headlights appeared on the horizon and he squinted against darkness broken only by distant stars. His blood slowed in his veins as his heart struggled with unanswered needs.

Danielle had come to him.

A red Camaro pulled into view and Jace's heart-beat quickened. Now that she was here, it was his chance to start a new life, their chance to start the next generation of Farrells.

Everything in his carefully constructed world was about to change. And as long as he kept his heart well guarded, the differences could only be for the better. Finally, the circle would be complete. He would have it all, including the social accep-tance that had been denied him so far. Danielle would open that last door for him—and give him the children he so desperately wanted.

Crossing his arms, Jace leaned against the porch railing, eager for the showdown he knew they were about to have.

The porch light enhanced her features as Danielle stepped out of the low-slung car. Her dark brown hair swirled around her head and shoulders in tight curls, and Jace experienced a pang of regret for the long tresses he used to enjoy so much. She groaned audibly as her heels sank into the thick mud he called a front yard.

Jace tugged his lips out of the grin pulling at the corners of his mouth. The scene was so familiar he could almost forget all that stood between them. Almost. "I see you remembered the way."

"In another lifetime, I made this drive daily."

He remembered. She would be waiting for him when he came in for the evening. Those moments after sunset became his favorite time of the day—because she was there.

But without warning, she'd moved to Denver. And evening had become a time of torture.

He tipped his head, ignoring the memory of past

loneliness that washed over him. "I thought I'd have to come get you."

She glared at him as she tried to draw herself free of the sucking mud. "You left me with few choices, Jace." Anger, frustration and a touch of hopelessness graced her fine features.

Jace shrugged, denying any sense of remorse. "There are always choices, Danielle." He let her battle the mud for a long minute. "Let me help you inside. It's muddy out here." He made the offer even though he knew she would refuse.

She lifted one foot, looking like a finicky kitten, and glared at him. "So what else is new? It's either muddy or rock hard. Either way, I always ruined my heels whenever I came here."

"That's why we wear boots in the real West, ma'am." He stretched his words into an exaggerated drawl and tipped his hat. When he started forward, she held up a hand.

"Don't. I'll make it to the porch by myself." She took one step forward, then lost her shoe to the clinging ooze when she tried to take another. Balancing on one foot, she looked up at Jace, resignation in her eyes.

In a few quick strides, he stood in front of her. She gingerly placed one hand on his shoulder to keep her balance; just that light touch ignited a fire deep within him. Her gaze dropped to the level of his chest and he knew it was costing her to let him help her, to let him touch her again. He knew it cost him—to be this close, to put his hands on her again, without making love to her.

Slipping an arm under her legs and another behind her back, he swept her against his chest, leaving both her shoes mired in the mud. The fire burned a little hotter. When he climbed the porch steps, she squirmed, heating his blood, too.

"I appreciate the caveman maneuvers, but you can put me down now." Her voice held a slight quiver. She wasn't unaffected by him, but then he'd already discovered that at the party.

"No, I can't. Your feet will get cold." He leaned forward, indicating she should push the door open. The warmth of the kitchen greeted them like an old friend.

After Danielle closed the door, he went to the large oak table that dominated the kitchen. He started to ease her into a chair, then stopped.

"No, not here." He crossed the room again, carrying her into the living room. The darkness didn't slow him. He'd lived in this house too many years to have any doubts about where things were.

Shadows surrounded them, camouflaging the bitterness. Danielle's muscles slowly loosened as she relaxed. He was overly aware of the soft wool of her sweater tickling his arms, the silk of her hair as it brushed against his neck.

She sighed, her breath sweeping across his face. "Put me down, Jace." Her voice carried all the pain, all the emotional baggage, that still stood between them.

"Why?"

"I came here to talk, nothing more."

Her anguish and exhaustion tore at him.

"Jace, please."

He slipped his arm from under her legs, letting them slide downward. But he held her close, her feet not quite touching the floor as he savored her.

She grabbed at his shoulders to steady herself, then tried to pull away.

"Let me go."

How could he let her go now? How could he step away from her when all he wanted was to lay her on the floor and discover the changes eleven years had made to her body?

"Kiss me first." He loosened his grip until her toes rested on the floor.

"Don't do this, Jace." Her head dropped forward, her forehead leaning against his shoulder.

"Kiss me, Dani. Prove to me it's over. Prove your feelings for me are dead."

He waited with anticipation, but she didn't move. "I dare you."

Lifting her head, she stretched upward and brushed her mouth against his. "There, see? I'm totally unaffected."

"That's not a kiss, Dani. Really kiss me. Or doesn't Raymond like that kind of thing?" He was taunting her, he knew, but desire had surged through him with an almost overpowering strength when her breasts slid against his chest. He needed to know she felt at least a small measure of the same.

Because desire was all there would ever be between them.

His heart ticked off the seconds. She edged closer until their lips touched. With a small groan, she pressed her mouth against his. Heat swept over him, weakening his knees. Bracing his legs farther apart, he held her closer, trying to force away the overwhelming sensations. But when her tongue darted out to wet his lips, he lost control.

A low growl vibrated his throat as he bent one knee, never breaking the contact of their lips. He eased Danielle to the rug in front of the cold fireplace, cradling her in his arms as he wished for the glow of flickering flames to bathe her skin when he peeled off her clothes. His hand swept the length of her before returning to stroke the side of her breast.

When his fingers brushed against the softness he craved to touch, Danielle jerked away. "No." She pulled her arms from his neck and pushed against his chest.

Jace held her fast, trying to sort through her conflicting messages. But when she pinched him on the tender skin under his arm, he jumped away, dumping her to the floor with little ceremony.

"Damn, woman. You sure know how to end a moment." He massaged his arm as he glared at her.

"Don't touch me again, Jace, or else."

Even in the muted darkness, he saw the anger sparkling in her green eyes, an anger that could spark the cold control he was fighting to retain. "That could make it difficult to have children after we're married."

Silence grew between them, a silence that made Jace wonder if he had underestimated Danielle.

"I haven't said I'll marry you."

When her gaze darted away from his, he read the bravado in her words and relaxed. She was in no position to refuse him and they both knew it. Still, he couldn't resist tormenting her. "Yet." She grabbed a pillow off the couch and threw it at his head. Jace caught it easily, holding it out to examine. "We used to have some great pillow fights. Remember? And the loser always had to—"

"That part of our relationship is over."

"Last I checked, we didn't have a relationship. But I suspect you're about to make me an offer I can't refuse. I'll go make us some coffee while you...plan how you're going to win me over."

He stood, trying not to grin at her anger. At least he'd proven one thing. She wasn't immune to him. Danielle wanted him as much as he wanted her. And once they were married, he could use that desire, use it to get the family he wanted and the revenge he needed.

He had five minutes alone in the kitchen before she joined him. Five minutes to wonder if he should have done something differently. He would give half his land to know what had gone through her head while she sat in the other room alone.

When she finally entered the kitchen, her mask of control was back in place. Danielle didn't look at him, didn't speak. Her nylon-clad feet made no sound on the well-worn oak floor as she wandered the room, her fingers brushing against things that still had to be familiar. She stopped in front of the old kitchen clock they'd discovered in a junk store, the one where the cat's tail twitched in time to the second hand.

Jace felt a twinge of loneliness. That had been a magical day, one of many good times they'd had when they were together. That clock represented the one tangible reminder of her, of their time together, that he just hadn't been able to dispose of.

Danielle finally settled by the back door, staring outside. Jace sensed a change in her, sensed something was about to happen. He forced himself to quietly drink his coffee and give her the time she needed, but anticipation coiled in his stomach.

Soon—very soon—she would be his again.

The cat's tail twitched at least another hundred times before she spoke.

"I don't want to marry you, Jace."

The coffee mug started to slip from his fingers and Jace barely caught it. Of everything he'd expected her to say, this wasn't it. He carefully set his cup on the counter.

"Excuse me?" He'd expected a skirmish, some token resistance. But not this—not an outright refusal.

She turned to face him, raising her chin and squaring her shoulders. *"I don't want to marry you."*

He wouldn't panic, wouldn't let her see just how deeply her words had affected him. His little Dani girl had grown up. And he wasn't certain she would respond to the threats he could make. Shrugging, he tried to placate her. "I won't make a bad husband, Danielle. I won't force you to scrub the floors or slop the hogs or feed the chickens. Your only job will be to warm my bed." He paused to let his words soak in. "Often."

Color flared into her cheeks.

"You did understand that, didn't you? I don't just want a dress-up doll for a wife. I want all the trimmings, all the privileges—and a family, too." He stepped closer to make certain she understood him. "I want forever."

The pink stains drained from her cheeks and her eyes widened. "But you don't love me."

Something shifted deep inside him, but he forced himself to ignore it. "A good marriage doesn't require love."

She flinched at his cruel words, but he could see she was wavering and he crowded her space even more. She took a half step back and met with the wall, her palms flattening against the painted surface.

He traced her jawline with his finger, reveled in the softness of her skin. Soon, he would possess her body again. Soon, she would be his.

When her throat moved in a soft gulp, he stroked her neck, then dipped one finger inside the neckline of her sweater. "Take it off."

She gasped and shrank away from him, but he planted both hands against the wall on each side of her.

"It's over, Danielle. Take it off."

Anger sparked her green eyes and she stiffened. "I'm not undressing for you."

A stab of heat flashed through him and his physical reaction was immediate and obvious. Struggling for control, he waited to voice his response. Finally, he raised his left hand and waved his fingers. "That rock on your finger? It's not mine."

Danielle looked down at her hand as if she'd forgotten what it looked like. Her lips tightening, she twisted the ring off, then held it in her palm, glaring at it.

"I...I don't want..." She finally met his eyes, her own shadowed with doubts.

His jaw tightened, then he forced himself to relax. "What you need is a roommate and a bundle of cash to save your father, right?"

"It could work, Jace. And there would be no complications for us to deal with."

"I have no problem with that." He waited until she looked up at him. "During the day."

"But—"

"At night, we *will* share a bedroom. And a bed." He leaned closer, until the scent of her perfume filled his head and her hair brushed against his cheek. "At night, you'll be my wife in every sense of the word." She gasped, but the sound only stirred his senses to a higher pitch. "And I promise you, you'll enjoy every moment."

Danielle ducked under his arm and darted across the room. Her hands shook slightly as she took down a coffee cup, only spilling a few drops of the brew when she poured. Taking several sips, she fingered the locket at her throat, letting her gaze settle everywhere in the room but on him.

"Fine. I'll even sleep with you. I'll pretend to be the perfect wife. But I won't make love with you." Her voice hardened with determination. "I won't have sex with a man who doesn't love me." She shook her hair back and raised her chin. "That's all it would be between us, Jace. Just sex. No emotions, no feelings, nothing but a physical release."

Anger surged through him. He knew how she responded to him, to his touch. He knew he could make her melt in his arms. She couldn't deny the physical chemistry that sparked between them. "I'm supposed to lie next to you night after night and never touch you?" He snorted his disgust at her idea. "I'm not a Boy Scout, Danielle. I'm a man."

She had the grace to look a little guilty. But she

still had the strength left to argue with him. "And I'm not the kind of woman to sell her body."

Silence throbbed between them.

Jace struggled to control his icy rage at her words. Without thinking, without realizing the consequences, he struck back. "If I remember correctly, your daddy needs money, over a million dollars. And you were perfectly willing to sell your body to Raymond. When I arrived at the party, you even managed to look like you were enjoying his attentions." Jace dropped his voice to a husky threat. "But I know something Raymond doesn't know. I know how to make you burn in my arms."

Pausing, Jace watched as the color drained from her face. Guilt tweaked at his conscience, but he almost had what he'd dreamed of for eleven years and he wasn't about to let up now.

"And I know how to keep your daddy from getting the money he so desperately needs."

"Don't threaten me."

Danielle's voice trembled with the emotions building inside her. Jace knew the explosion was coming, knew he would get burned, but he chose to ignore it. "If you don't marry me, Danielle, I'll make damn sure no other man will have you. It was easy enough to get rid of Raymond. Do you honestly think I'd find it difficult to get rid of any other marriage candidates?"

He waited, certain she would give in. She had no choice. Victory hovered just a breath away.

"No, Jace." Her lips tightened, turning almost white with her anger. "I've changed my mind. I'll find another way."

"There is no other way." Needing some time to

regroup, Jace stuffed his hands into the back pockets of his blue jeans and went to stare out the kitchen window. He was too close. He couldn't let her go now.

To match his deteriorating mood, dark clouds rolled in from the west, threatening an early snow. He frowned, briefly considering the extra work and longer hours a storm would bring.

Frustration welled up inside him and his teeth ached from the pressure exerted by his jaw. Getting Danielle back into his life wasn't supposed to be this difficult. But he wouldn't give up. He needed his revenge against Simmons, needed to hold Danielle again. By Jace's thinking, everyone would win with their marriage, but the Simmons family would still pay their debt.

As if on cue, flakes of snow began to slowly drift to the ground.

He needed time, space, a chance to plan a new attack. With his back still to Danielle, he said, "You'd better leave before the snow starts to stick. That little race car of yours will be worthless once the roads ice up."

"I'm not going anywhere until we get this resolved."

He didn't have to turn around to know her chin had come up while she braced for a battle. And he refused to accept defeat. Since threats hadn't worked, maybe it was time to turn on the charm. Jace softened his voice and his stance. "I can help you—you and your family. And I'm not asking for much in return."

"Just my soul."

Jace winced as her words knifed through him.

But he refused to retreat. "We can help each other."

"Like you helped me last night?" Danielle bit her lip. "You should have stuck around, watched the fireworks." Her laugh was tinged with bitterness. "You would have enjoyed the show, I'm sure." Tears swam in her eyes, but she blinked hard, refusing to let them fall. "After Raymond left the party, Daddy sent everyone home. The looks they gave me..."

She struggled to draw a deep breath. "Daddy called me a failure, said I couldn't even manage to hold a man." She brushed angrily at the one tear that dared escape. "And I guess he's right."

Jace moved closer, willing to offer comfort. "I'll never consider you a failure. I've seen what you can do when you set your mind to it. Marry me, Danielle. Marry me and prove your father wrong. Together, we can build a good life together."

She gulped. "Do you really think that's possible?" Her voice echoed her disbelief.

"Anything is possible. I've had to prove that several times these past years."

He waited, let her absorb his words. Then he ruined it all. But the words had to be said. He couldn't deceive her in that way.

"I'll never love you," Jace said. A shaft of guilt stabbed him when her eyes darkened with pain. "You walked away once. I can't give you my heart again. But we can make a nice enough life together. As long as you don't fight me at every turn and you understand why you're here."

"I walked away?"

"Ran is more like it. And never once did you

look back.'' The days after she'd left town still haunted him. But her rejection had also been the secret to his achievements. Anger had fueled his desire to succeed and combined with it to make a potent potion. Whenever he felt discouraged, all he'd had to do was remember.

Danielle moved toward him, her expression unreadable. Jace resisted the urge to draw away. She reached up and stroked her fingers across the dark shadow of his beard, the rasping sound bringing on a new set of memories.

A flicker of hope flared inside Jace. Maybe, by some miracle, he stood a chance of winning. Maybe she would give in and they could go to bed. Together.

Suddenly, he was bone weary, tired of the fighting, the struggling. All he wanted was to make love to her, then fall asleep with her in his arms.

Danielle leaned closer, just close enough for him to catch the teasing scent of her perfume again.

''I despise you.''

The carefully enunciated words vibrated through the room as she pushed past him and walked away.

# Chapter Three

She'd lied.

She could never hate Jace, even after he'd spurned her love and traded a lifetime with her for the temptation of money.

But she wanted to hate him. And someway, she was going to have to learn how. Because right now, he could hurt her again. Hate was the only thing that might protect her. Her pride had been wounded by Raymond's callous rejection, her heart almost shattered by her father's anger. If Jace offered her just a crumb of warmth, she would fall in love with him all over again.

She had to protect herself against the indomitable force that was Jace. Hugging her arms around herself as she entered the living room, she slowly sank to the floor and tried to silence her torrential thoughts.

Slipping Raymond's ring into her pocket, she closed that chapter of her life. Danielle raised her left hand to study it, a frown pulling at her forehead. Why did her hand suddenly feel so light, so free? Why did the weight of her problems seem to diminish with the removal of the two-karat diamond? She'd simply traded one set of disasters for another.

But for now, there was an odd acceptance in her, as if she'd known all along this was how it was going to end. In spite of her brave words, she would have to marry Jace. If the two of them could find a middle ground to share, they just might manage to build a contented life together. That image was probably more fairy tale than reality, but she needed to cling to the idea that they would be happy.

Dropping her left hand in her lap, she massaged her forehead with the right, trying to ease the headache building there.

When she'd driven up to the ranch tonight, the shadow of his hat had concealed Jace's expression. But she didn't have to see him to know his eyes reflected wariness and a deep, quiet anger. The only time he'd ever allowed himself a measure of any other emotion had been during their lovemaking. But even that had been a small allowance, only what he was willing to let her see.

Her breasts tightened and warmth pooled in her stomach as she remembered the nights she'd spent in this house, snuggled in Jace's big four-poster bed, wrapped in his arms.

Warm, protected, cared for. All hers simply for the asking when Jace had wanted her. For the first time in her life, she hadn't experienced the lonely ache in her heart that had started the day her mother had walked away.

Without warning, that tenderness had been ripped

away from her. When she'd lost Jace, the pain had been so powerful, she'd simply built a wall around her heart and made the decision not to love again. Ever.

After so many years of being on her own, she'd decided friendship would be enough to keep her happy. She'd thought once she was married to Raymond, she'd be safe. But Jace had interfered. As usual. And now she wasn't certain she'd ever be safe again.

Jace took what he wanted from life and he was rarely denied. She'd seen that over and over as she'd followed his business successes in the newspapers her father had sent her. Danielle closed her eyes, trying to block the memories, but they flooded through her with too much force to be stopped.

From the first time he'd seen her, he'd pursued her with single-minded purpose.

Her first solo effort at entertaining had been at the age of nineteen. Everything had to be perfect so her daddy would be proud.

It had been a large party, with too many people whom Danielle had never met. They were her father's acquaintances, business contacts and people who could further his investments.

But having been raised to perform as the consummate hostess, she smiled, shook hands and made small talk until her jaw ached. The evening stretched interminably ahead. She was bored, her feet hurt, and she wanted to go to bed. Until she sensed *him* watching her.

First her skin tingled, then she felt a gaze on her back, stroking like a gentle caress. A shiver shuddered through her as the gaze insistently urged her to turn around.

When she did, the intense blue of his eyes captured her attention and scattered all thoughts of her responsibilities. Heat poured through her limbs, leaving her weak, disoriented. Shaken by her immediate reaction to the stranger, she wandered away from the conversation around her without a word of excuse.

Suddenly, she felt the need for a drink. Not normally one to indulge in alcohol at these gatherings, she snagged a glass of champagne from the first waiter she passed and headed toward the fresh air beckoning from the open patio doors. The man was moving closer, seeking her out, and Danielle sensed there was nothing she could do to avoid him. She wasn't certain she even wanted to try.

A soft touch brushed against her shoulder.

"Mind if I join you, ma'am?" The husky drawl stroked across her skin like a trickle of warm sand.

She turned slowly, warily, knowing what that gaze could do to her. Sucking in a deep breath, she tried to speak normally. "What can I do for you, Mr....?"

"Farrell, ma'am. Jace Farrell."

He'd been twenty-two years old and full of confidence—a confidence that enveloped her and made her believe anything was possible.

He took her elbow and guided her to the open French doors. Once on the porch, he turned away from the couples gathered there and managed to find a secluded corner shadowed by a thicket of trees.

She leaned against the rail and waited, anticipation sifting through her.

He didn't run his gaze over the length of her body the way most men did when they met her. His eyes never wavered, never looked away from hers. He seemed to be trying to get inside her emotions, to get to know her without taking the time for small talk.

She returned his stare, determined not to be intimidated, but the need to retreat was almost overwhelming as the silence stretched between them.

"You'll be sharing my bed before the month is over."

She gasped at his wild assertion, the sudden breath tangling in her throat. The man was more than a shade crazy. She edged backward, only to be halted by the porch railing.

"And you'll be my wife before the end of the year."

She should have laughed in his face. Or thrown her champagne at him. Instead, she felt tingling excitement shoot through her, lighting her blood like a Fourth of July sparkler.

"Mr. Farrell, I—"

"I know." His lips lifted into a grin. "I sound a bit loco. But I always know what I want when I see it." The smile faded as he moved closer, his mouth almost touching hers, his breath stroking her face. "I want you. And I always get what I want."

He didn't kiss her. Instead, he smoothed his finger across her lips and withdrew. But Danielle felt like she'd been branded. He pulled her hand into his and led her inside as if knowing just how much he tempted her. Her body reacted to him with a white heat that threatened her composure. She wanted him to touch her again...and again...so this flaring excitement would never dissipate.

He stayed with her the remainder of the evening, tactfully extracting her from lengthy conversations, following her to the kitchen while she checked on the food, making certain there was always a full glass of champagne in her hand. His fingers drifted at the small of her back as he guided her gently with a touch to her elbow, never satisfying her growing need, always leaving her hungering for more.

Later, she tried to blame the champagne. But deep down inside, she knew different. *He* was different. He was dangerous. And she couldn't resist the chance to play with the fire sparking between them.

As the evening drew to a triumphant close, he pulled her aside. Trapping her against the wall with his lean length, he smiled, a slow, seductive twist of his lips, before asking, "May I buy you a cup of coffee, ma'am?"

She'd been lost ever since.

"May I buy you a cup of coffee, ma'am?"

The words echoed through her thoughts and it took a moment to realize Jace was standing beside her, a mug of coffee in each hand.

She glanced at the black leather furniture in the rugged room. She was no longer at her home, finishing up a major function as her daddy's hostess while trying to fight off a shocking attraction to a totally unsuitable man. She was in Jace's home, listening to the wind build outside, surrounded by rough log walls, masculine furniture and Southwestern artifacts.

And she'd just declared she despised the man she was destined to marry.

Her fingers trembling slightly, she grabbed at the mug like a lifeline and took a quick sip, hoping the caffeine would help clear the past from her mind.

It was over. All of it. She needed to hang on to that. Love wasn't possible between her and Jace, at least not a mutual love. She needed to remember the purpose of her marriage to him. It was little more than a business arrangement and she needed to keep her distance. It was the only way she could maintain her sanity.

Jace set down his coffee and turned to the fireplace. "Do you want to talk about it?"

She froze, the mug halfway to her mouth. Jace wanting to talk? Wanting to know what she thought? A bitter laugh almost escaped. This was something to be noted down in her book of firsts. But in spite of this shocking new turn, she wasn't ready to bare her soul. At least not to Jace Farrell. She might never be ready. "No."

Jace shrugged, apparently unconcerned by her response. "Snow's getting bad, so you might as well spend the night. I wouldn't want you to get stuck in that fancy little car. The plows might not dig you out for days."

Danielle swiped at the dark circles she knew were rimming her eyes. A few days of isolation would be heavenly. If only it could be with anyone else but Jace.

From the moment her father had called three months ago asking for her help, she hadn't slept well. Before, her life had been so simple. She'd been working her way up the corporate ladder at a midsize investment firm in Denver. It was difficult being away from home, but she'd been trying to learn everything she could for the day when her father let her join him in the family company which held widespread investments in land, restaurants, and banking. Now, she was setting herself up as a full-time bought-and-paid-for wife.

She watched Jace build the fire, enjoying the play of muscles in his back—a back that was broader, harder than before. When he'd held her last night, it was as if no time had passed between them. Even after all these years, she hadn't convinced her body not to want him. The old memories tried crowding into her mind, but she shoved them away.

All but one recollection obligingly faded.

He'd said he wanted to marry her, take her as his wife.

It had all been part of his deception to get the money he needed for his ranch.

By this time, if everything had gone according to his plans, they would have been married for over ten years, would probably have had several children. And she still might not know the truth. Because she'd been so in love with him, so wrapped up in their future together, she hadn't noticed the little things that showed his true feelings.

Pain lanced through her at the memories, the hopes, the dreams they'd shared.

But it was too late for that fairy tale. Now, they would still be married, but there would be no love given...or taken. Jace wanted her physically, but she needed more from him. She needed all of him, his heart included. But his heart wasn't part of the deal.

Danielle squeezed her eyes shut. Heaven help her, but she hoped she was doing the right thing. Jace held so much power over her emotions. She had spent the past twenty-four hours desperately searching for another way to help her father. But Jace was the only knight available—and his armor was tarnished.

"Your predictions were wrong," she whispered as the sound of a striking match punctuated her words.

"What predictions?"

"We didn't marry within the year." The past pierced her heart.

"But you *were* in my bed the next week." He set flame to the newspaper as easily as he'd set flame to her body. In bed with him, she'd reveled in her newfound sensuality. He'd been her first lover, had taught her well, had taught her to enjoy her own body...and his.

Did he remember, too? Did it keep him awake at night until he thought he'd die of longing? That night had been pure magic. But magic never lasted forever. It tended to fade in the cold light of reality.

"That was only half of your prediction."

He turned to stare at her, the firelight casting his face in shadows.

"Well, darlin', you are going to marry me."

"But it won't be a real marriage. We don't love each other." She took another gulp of coffee, barely noticing as it burned her tongue. Maybe the sting would remind her not to let herself be burned twice by passion's flames.

"It'll be real enough." Jace stood, his movements powerful, and walked over to join her. He sat right next to her, rather than backing off to the corner like most people would. But then Jace rarely acted like most people.

Fidgeting with her mug, she waited. His leg brushed against hers. She scooted over a few inches. The fire popped, and she felt Jace studying her, but she refused to look up. Long seconds passed by, then he moved closer again, his body heat penetrating her clothing and warming her thigh.

"So." She wet her lips and gulped a mouthful of coffee. "Where do we start?"

He shrugged, staring into the orange flames. "You hate me, hate what I'm doing. At least that's out in the open."

She dissected his words, his tone, trying to discover what he was feeling, but she couldn't tell a thing. Reminding herself of her father's situation, she forced the proper words to her lips. "I shouldn't have said that. I'm sorry."

"No, you're not."

She'd have to be cautious. He could still read her every thought before she'd even expressed it. Danielle tried to rein in her racing mind long enough to form an answer. When she didn't respond, he stood and went upstairs, leaving her to struggle alone with her doubts.

A few minutes later, he returned and dropped something into her lap. "You'll need a ring to make this official."

Danielle stared at the glittering diamond ring with a sense of helpless wonder. "You saved it?"

Her voice barely reached the level of a whisper. Emotion threatened to choke her as she dared to hope that he might have cared more than he'd ever admit.

"The stones were too small to make it worth selling, so I kept it to remind me of what could happen if I wasn't careful."

Her wonder deflated with a painful whoosh and she closed her eyes against the agony his words caused.

"Put it on. I'm sure it will fit."

She clamped her lips together. She wanted to lash out at him, to hurt him. But she was smart enough to know that he would win any battle of wits and she would only end up making herself miserable. Maybe if she played the game, she could tame him just enough to make their life together bearable.

She buried her wants and needs deep in her heart. The marriage was inevitable. No matter which way she turned, there was no other way to help her father. She knew that once Jace set his mind on something, he would get it. And right now, for whatever reason, he wanted her.

"Will you do the honors?" She held out the ring, pleading silently that he make an effort.

"I suppose you want me to get down on one knee, too?"

She forced a smile to her lips, determined to make this into a special moment. "It would be a nice gesture, but it's not necessary. You already did that part once."

In fact, the night he'd bought her that ring had been the most romantic night of her life. It would be a wonderful memory to cling to when the days grew too cold and lonely. At least her nights wouldn't be spent in isolation. Her blood heated at the thought of sharing a bed with Jace again.

He snatched the ring from her grasp and grabbed her left hand. At her soft gasp, he gentled his grip and carefully slid the ring on her finger. Very slowly, as if giving her time to escape, he bent his head toward hers. Just before their lips touched, he spoke. "You're mine, Danielle. And I don't share."

Danielle gulped, unable to think of the sensible response with him so near. Instead, the wrong words crowded to her lips, words that needed to be said. "You promise to help my father?"

He hesitated, his mouth a breath away from hers, and she could feel the anger building inside him. Regret washed over her, regret that she'd spoiled the moment by bringing up the reason for their marriage. But she had to be certain.

His mouth met hers and she whimpered as his heat washed over her. He reached for her shoulders and propelled her against the back of the couch, never breaking the contact. His tongue swept over her lips, demanding entry into her mouth, but she pressed them tightly together.

When he softened the kiss to heartbreaking sweetness, she tried to twist away. But he held her, coaxing a response. It became a battle of wills to see who would win this contest. Danielle was determined to make her point. She wouldn't keep her part of the bargain until he promised to keep his.

Finally, Jace broke away, his breathing labored as he leaned back to glare at her. He quirked one eyebrow. "Denying me my rights already?"

Danielle resisted the urge to wipe away the deceit

of that kiss and returned his glare. "We aren't married yet. And I'm not denying you a thing." She stood and walked over to the fire, needing distance between them. "I'll be your wife and I'll share your bed. That was the deal." She closed her eyes, needing to shut out the image of his muscular body lounging against the black leather, a predatory wariness surrounding him. "But not until after the wedding."

"Then I may as well go to bed. Alone." As he left the room, he paused on the third step and turned to her. "I had planned to make an effort at romance tonight. I thought it would make the whole thing easier on you. But you're right. Why mix business with pleasure?" He let the silence build between them. "I'm sure you remember where the guest room is."

With those final words, he left her to sort through her feelings. Seeking the familiar, she threaded her fingers through the gold chain around her neck. Regret curled through her as he disappeared from view. They were going to need some rules in order to survive this marriage.

As she brushed her hair from her face, the diamond winked. She raised her hand, surprised how heavily the ring weighed on her finger. The first time she'd worn it, the ring had represented a promise of a bright, happy future. Raymond's ring had been more like the weighty burden of safety and security. But now, with Jace's diamond once again on her finger, all she had was a cold, glittering reminder of all she'd lost and all she'd never have. It didn't bear thinking about.

Slowly, she followed him up the stairs. The wind

rattled around the house, reminding her of just how alone she was. When she reached the top, she hesitated, contemplating the closed door of Jace's bedroom. Had she made the wrong choice? It probably didn't matter whether they waited for a wedding to sleep together, but it was important to her. She needed to exert some control over her life, over their relationship, and this was one small matter she had a say in.

Walking past temptation, she entered the barren coldness of the guest room. Other than a few pieces of furniture and a handmade quilt on the bed, there was little to welcome her. But then, to her knowledge, few people ever visited Jace.

Over the years, she'd never heard rumors of affairs or women, so if he'd had either, he'd been very discreet. Jealousy flooded through her when she pictured another woman in Jace's arms, another woman in his bed. He was a passionate man, a demanding lover, and she couldn't imagine him being totally alone all this time.

Her own memories of him, of his lovemaking, were so clear, so real. If she gave her body over to him now, she was afraid the relationship would consume her. Somehow she had to delay the physical side of the marriage, had to make Jace see that they needed to learn more about each other before they slept together.

The barren silence surrounded her, broken only by the lonely wind, and she knew there would be no sleep for her the way things stood. She had to try to reason with him once more.

Before common sense could prevail, Danielle retraced her path down the hall. Her knock was hesitant, his answer a long time in coming. Rather than barge in on him, she called through the door.

"We need to talk, Jace."

Again, silence.

"We'll talk in the morning."

"Please, Jace."

Finally, he invited her in.

She halted in the doorway, surprised to see that absolutely nothing had changed in the years she'd been away. The same handmade quilt covered the bed, the same oak furniture added a warm touch, and the same Southwestern art pieces still decorated the room.

And Jace, bare-chested, sat in the four-poster bed, sheets pulled up to his waist, looking as impossibly virile as ever.

Her breath froze in her throat as she was confronted with his masculine aura. Temptation flickered through her—to drop her clothes and join him, to absorb his heat and let him make love to her— but she quickly squashed it. To go to him now out of an emotional need would only hurt her in the end.

Jace put aside the magazine he'd been reading and crossed his arms. "What's so important that it couldn't wait until morning?"

"I don't want to end the evening like this. We still need to talk, to sort things out."

He sighed and ran his hand through his hair, his shoulders slumping slightly. "Would it be any different from before, Dani? Or would we just ignore the real issue and never resolve anything?"

Danielle smoothed her hands down her slacks, desperately wanting something to occupy her fingers. "Nothing has changed, so I imagine it'll be the same territory as before."

She waited for his answer. But none came. She tried to push away the anger and remember that she needed his help.

"Jace, I can't turn my feelings on and off like a faucet. What we had is over and we have to begin another relationship now, one based on friendship rather than sex."

He threw the covers aside and leaped from the bed, coming to a stop just inches away from her. Danielle forced her gaze away from his hard chest, ordered her eyes not to drift downward to where a pair of sweatpants hung low on his hips.

"You think we can live together and just be roommates?"

Slowly, she nodded, knowing she was lying to herself and to him.

"And my return for paying off your father's debts is to gain a friend?"

She couldn't even answer his question this time.

His voice dropped to a low growl. "Can you live the rest of your life without a man kissing you? Without a man making you whimper with need? Without a man making you cry out when all the passion breaks loose inside you?"

She stared at him, a thousand images crashing through her thoughts, images of Jace, stroking, kissing, making her crazy with longing. The smoldering heat inside her burst into flames.

His voice dropped to a ragged whisper. "Can you, Dani girl?"

She tried to step away, terrified of her feelings, tried to escape the burning intensity in his eyes. "I don't need..." She couldn't finish, couldn't admit the truth. Not to Jace.

"You need, Dani. Just like the rest of us mortals." He grasped her shoulders, shook her gently. "Admit it." His voice deepened to a growl of frustration.

"There's more to a relationship than sex. We can have a very good marriage, be the best of friends without sleeping together."

He laughed.

The full, rich sound of his voice filled the room. She'd have slapped him just for the satisfaction, but she couldn't raise her hand. He had no right to belittle her, no right to judge her.

She squirmed against his grip.

Jace's grin widened.

"That's enough."

"You're so naive, Danielle."

Anger flooded through her, giving her the strength to break away. Rubbing her arms in agitation, she looked around the room, her gaze desperately searching for something to look at besides the tempting expanse of Jace's chest. "I can't stay here. I'll take my chances with the snowstorm."

She should have made a grand exit, but she couldn't resist one last look to see his reaction. He didn't respond. He was standing with his hands propped on his hips, head dropped forward as if he was deep in thought.

The picture he presented was so out of character, she stopped. "Jace?"

His chest heaved as he dragged air into his lungs. "I'm sorry, Dani. I had no right to say that."

Surprised by his apology, she simply stared. Jace Farrell had never apologized to her before.

When she started to answer, he stepped closer and gently laid his finger across her lips. "Stay, Dani girl." He traced her mouth, leaving a path of enticement. "We *will* be husband and wife. The rest will take care of itself."

Finally, admitting defeat, she nodded in agreement.

"Sleep with me?"

She was tempted, so tempted. She needed his strength, his confidence, his energy, tonight. She needed to feel loved and special.

The words almost choked her. "I can't."

He simply nodded and moved away. She stared at him for what seemed an eternity, waged a silent, internal battle and finally found the courage to step into the hallway, closing the door behind her.

A flood of dread filled Danielle as she realized that she'd only made her situation much worse. She'd thought she could control the old feelings for Jace, that she could relegate their past to a simple physical need and ignore it.

But she couldn't.

# Chapter Four

Danielle slowly stretched each muscle, feeling only warmth and contentment in her cocoon of blankets. Soon, she would be Mrs. Jace Farrell. Soon, she would have his loving twenty-four hours a day instead of just when they could squeeze in a moment for each other.

Her toes connected with a cold, empty space—a space where she'd expected to find Jace. It was then that reality burst her dream world.

She'd dreamed of their past, of the way things used to be between them.

Burying her head in the pillow, she groaned. Going downstairs this morning would be much worse than the typical morning after.

Waking up next to Jace had always been filled with laughing and loving. When they'd first become lovers, there had been no awkwardness between them. But then, she'd been nineteen years old and thought herself madly in love with the man she'd planned to spend the rest of her life with.

This morning would be different. Their past, their anger and a singing tension would hover between them.

Danielle glared at the watery gray light seeping through the curtains. Her mind wasn't helping matters one bit. During the night, her dreams had been very vivid...and very explicit.

But totally unsatisfying.

The time she'd spent with her dream version of Jace had been magical, more than she'd thought possible between a man and a woman. And it left her aching. If the real-life Jace managed to read the remnants of her night fantasies on her face, he'd realize just how much power he held over her.

In spite of their past, of the pain he'd caused her, she wanted him. She tried to change the direction of her thoughts, but there was only one other question lurking in her brain.

Was she doing the right thing? Did she dare risk a lifetime with Jace? Did she have any other options?

The doubts chased around in her head until she was forced from the security of the bed.

Wincing as her feet touched the cold floor, she hurried to pull on the same clothes she'd arrived in last night. The soft wool slacks always looked good, but she'd never put them through a two-day test before. The matching hunter-green sweater would at least keep her warm. Not finding her shoes, she hoped Jace had brought them in from the mud-filled yard.

She glared at her image in the bathroom mirror.

There was an emergency supply of makeup in her purse, but not enough to mask the dark circles shadowing her eyes, not enough to convince Jace her emotions were untouched.

She smoothed the taupe-colored shadow onto one eyelid. Last night when she'd arrived at the ranch, she'd honestly believed she could convince Jace that marriage would be a mistake and still find a way to ask him to lend her the money.

She hadn't arrived prepared to spend the night. And even though she'd been in Denver for over ten years, she should have remembered how quickly a late storm could trap the unprepared in Wyoming.

But she would have plenty of time to remember.

From this day on, her path was set and she saw no way out. She needed to hide her doubts and fears from him.

Trying to dismiss the haunting memories of the night, she concentrated on planning her day. First, she needed to see if the roads were clear. If she could get to the highway, she could make it home— home where she would be safe for a little while longer. At least until Jace decided it was time for them to marry.

Danielle froze when she touched the necklace at her throat. Her father would be furious. A cold chill of foreboding skidded down her spine.

But he was the one who'd concocted the idea of an arranged marriage. Raymond had been willing to pay well for a wife—and of course, a partnership in the company. Why should it matter who was the groom?

Because Jace had hurt her once. Hurt her badly.

And Tyrone Simmons didn't forgive easily when it came to his daughter's happiness.

If only Jace loved her, cared for her even a little bit. If only he weren't so bitter about the past.

She had resigned herself to a loveless union with Raymond, one in which friendship and mutual respect would be the basis of their relationship. Her heart had been shattered before and she had vowed then never to risk love again.

Marriage to Raymond would have been better than coming home to an empty apartment every night, preferable to being alone for the rest of her life. She had known him for years as a business acquaintance, had been comfortable with him. And she'd have helped her father in the process. Danielle had even allowed herself to dream of having a family.

Now, all that was impossible.

If she could control her desires, a marriage to Jace would be no different. The flutter of her pulse at the thought of his touch mocked her.

She went to the window, hoping for distraction, but nothing more than a wide expanse of white greeted her. There were a few tracks in the snow, snowmobiles probably, but nothing else to break the vast white wasteland. Shivering, she let the curtain drop back into place.

Maybe she wouldn't get home today. Maybe she would be stuck here, forced to deal with the power of Jace's determination. At least the snow gave her time to negotiate the business side of her arrangement with Jace. As soon as she received his check for the amount of the loan, she would deposit the money in her father's business account, then start planning the promised deed.

A deed that felt like a life sentence.

With a sigh, she wondered just how long she could delay this marriage. Even Jace would understand that it took time to plan a society wedding.

Danielle checked her makeup once more, sighing over her lack of supplies.

She hesitated with her hand on the doorknob.

Determined to make an effort at pleasantness, she tried to prepare herself to descend the stairs and greet Jace as if he truly was her fiancé.

So where was the rush of anticipation, the thrill of seeing him again? At one time, she had tingled just at the thought of him—had longed for him every moment they were separated. Today, all she felt was dread.

The battles between them were only beginning. And there would be battles because she wasn't going to just roll over and play dead to his masculine arrogance. Before they went any further with this charade, she needed to hear one promise from him.

He'd never committed to giving her the money her cooperation demanded. And she would have to find a way to control her temper until she had that money in hand. The important thing right now was to pay off the debt. Then she would find a way to deal with her marriage to a man who held the power to destroy the little bit of her heart that remained intact.

Pouring a much needed cup of coffee, Jace listened. When the bottom step of the stairway gave a warning creak, he turned in anticipation, the coffee cup halfway to his mouth.

His heart slammed to a stop.

And when the blood roared through his veins again, he doubted a gallon of pure caffeine could have a better effect.

She was beautiful.

The wounded shadows reflected in her eyes made his heart twist. The veneer of sophistication she normally wore like a suit of armor had disappeared overnight. Her tousled hair and lack of makeup gave her the look of an innocent.

He couldn't stop the memories, hadn't been able to all night. Introducing Danielle to the secrets of her body had changed his entire perspective on the art of making love. Those months they'd shared so many years ago had taught him more than he could ever hope to teach her.

And in spite of the old hurts, he wanted more.

She edged into the room. "Has the snow stopped?"

Jace swallowed his sigh. They hadn't indulged in small talk before, never talked about the weather. But at least for now, he would try. Maybe it would help put her at ease. He certainly didn't want a wife who jumped every time he walked into the room. Unless it was for all the right reasons.

"Yeah, but the roads are blocked by drifts."

"Any idea when they'll be clear?" Her eyes held a wary look.

He shook his head, memories halting any chance of speaking. The last time they were snowbound together, they'd taken full advantage of the time to explore each other's needs.

She took a step toward the coffeepot.

Finally, he took pity on her and moved out of her way. He would play the gentleman and give her a little while longer to adjust to their new relationship. But when she sipped her coffee and closed her eyes with a gentle sigh, all his good intentions landed in the snowdrift outside the back door.

As her eyelids slowly opened, her guard was down and he saw the almost sensual pleasure reflected in their green depths. Her lips parted slightly and he found himself battling his libido so he wouldn't cross the room and kiss her until that pleasure ignited into full-scale passion.

As soon as her gaze connected with his, the walls slid back into place.

"You haven't changed the house much since I was last here."

She had practically lived with him for the six months they'd been together. They'd both had commitments during the day, she to several charities, he to his fledgling ranch, but they'd met here every night.

And they had shared.

Cooking, cleaning, laughing, loving.

It had terrified him at the time just how much he needed her. And after he lost her, he'd vowed never to let another woman become that important to him. Not even Danielle. Because losing her had almost destroyed him. And his dreams.

So he shrugged away her comment. "No need to. I've always been satisfied with what I have."

"Then why do you need me?"

Her words landed a direct hit. She would never be allowed to know how badly he wanted her again.

Rather than let her see his reaction, he chose to turn her words around. "You're available, darlin'. And you owe me."

She stiffened and he could see the anger building inside her. He waited for the explosion, relishing a good fight. The night had left him aching and he needed a release for the tension simmering within him.

But he was disappointed.

The battle with her anger was tangible, but she finally claimed victory and turned away.

Silence ticked between them as she stared out the window. He wanted to know her thoughts, wanted to ask if she meant to honor her marriage vows. Was it possible to change those vows, make them even more binding?

Once he had her, he wouldn't give her up. For any reason.

"Did you sleep okay?" He winced at the mundane words. The faint bruising under her eyes gave visible testimony that she'd spent less time sleeping than he had. He wanted to ask if she'd dreamed of him, but he knew she'd never admit that she had. He consoled himself with the fact that he'd done everything in his power to insinuate himself into her dreams.

"I never sleep well in a strange bed."

"My bed used to be very familiar to you."

Her body pulled taut, but she didn't choose to answer. Jace searched for something else to say, then shrugged, wondering why he was trying. They had years ahead of them.

He turned to leave the kitchen, anxious to get the

ranch ready for his departure, but her words stopped him.

"When do you want the wedding?" There was a note of hesitation in her voice.

He had his plans, but he wasn't ready to share them yet. "Soon. And I want you to stay here until the ceremony."

"I have other commitments."

"You can't leave until the roads are plowed. Besides, I don't want *Daddy* spiriting you away before you have my ring on your finger."

"My father will honor any agreement I make."

"Right." She obviously didn't know what her father was capable of. But Jace did.

Pursing her lips, she went to the coffeepot. After refilling her cup, she stared into the rising steam. There was no sign of her reaction to his demand. He used to be able to read her every emotion. It saddened him to think that life had taught her to hide her feelings, to develop a hard outer shell.

"I'll need clothes." She turned slowly, her green eyes challenging, daring him to refuse.

The images came hard and fast. And in those images, she wasn't wearing any clothing. "No need to dress on my account." The blush that washed into her cheeks only made him want her more.

Her chin notched upward. "I'll need clothes," she repeated. "And I have no intention of staying here without anything more than what I have on."

"Pity." He gulped at the coffee, felt the burn all the way to his stomach and tried to force his thoughts to the business of running a ranch in a snowstorm. His men all knew their jobs and did them well, but he needed to make certain everything was dealt with before he left on their honeymoon.

*Honeymoon.*

The mere word sucked the breath from his lungs.

Soon. Very soon. She would belong to him again. Anticipation curled through him. And he would make certain that she enjoyed the nights so much that she wouldn't want to leave him.

"Jace?" She waved her fingers in front of his face. "My father has nothing to do with our agreement. I've said I'll marry you."

"I know you will. I won't allow you to back out."

"Then at least trust me enough to let me do what I need to."

"It's not you I don't trust."

She seemed to consider his words and he watched her carefully as she marshaled her next argument.

He pushed away from the counter. It was impossible to think with her so close. But when she followed him to the window, he had the sudden sensation of the hunter becoming the hunted. His legendary self-control slipped another fraction.

He forced himself to focus on what she was saying.

"If I go by the house this afternoon, Daddy won't be home from work yet. I can pack and be out of there before he realizes what's happened. I'll leave a note and the check, then come back here to stay with you."

He heard her words, absorbed them, then rejected them. But he wanted to see just how far she would take this fantasy.

"We can start planning the wedding and be married by the end of the month if you'd like." A faint tremor in her voice took the bravado from her words.

She pulled in a breath to continue with her plans. He watched as her breasts rose, molding gently into the green sweater she wore. And he knew he would die from wanting if he had to wait an entire month.

"No money until after the wedding."

Her breath caught, held, then escaped in a rush. "Jace, you know I need that money right away."

"Yes."

"By Friday."

He nodded.

"This is Tuesday." Her eyes widened as the trap closed around her. "But don't you want a big wedding? Something we can invite all our friends to?"

"No."

"But I need—"

"Danielle."

She froze.

"I want you." He let the silence stretch. "Now."

Not in the mood to be polite, he slammed down his coffee cup, dragged her close and absorbed the taste of her with his mouth. Her lips were still relaxed with surprise and he took full advantage, probing the depths of her sweet mouth with his tongue. Unable to stop his low groan, he pressed his hips against hers and tortured himself with the feel of her, so near and yet so far.

Desire flared through him like a freight train. Somehow finding the willpower, he released her and grabbed his coffee again, knowing he had to escape. "I have work to do." He stopped at the doorway. "We'll buy any clothing you need...on our honeymoon."

His last image was of Danielle sagging against the wall, her fingers hovering over her lips.

He silently cursed himself for a fool, using every foul word in his broad vocabulary. If he gave in to his need at every turn, she would quickly learn to use it against him. And he had every intention of being the one in control of their marriage.

Jace buried himself in his work, making certain everything was in order for him to leave. As soon as the roads were clear, he wanted to take Danielle away from Jackson for a few days. Her father was an unknown factor until they were bound by law. And there was still a remote chance she would change her mind.

Jace wasn't willing to take the risk. He had everything he wanted in the palm of his hand.

He left final instructions with his foreman, then dragged all the papers on his desk into a haphazard pile. He had one more thing to do before lunch.

His luck was holding. There was a lodge in the Grand Tetons where they'd stayed once before. And they just happened to have a luxury suite available for the next few nights. An elegant meeting room would serve perfectly as a chapel and a local minister was on call. Jace left detailed instructions for their arrival, then went to see what Danielle was up to.

The house had echoed with quiet all morning. If it hadn't been for the snow, he would've half expected her to try to run away. But the top of her car was barely visible over a snowdrift and he didn't think she was desperate enough to attempt the thirty-mile walk into town.

He found her in the kitchen, cooking. With raised eyebrows, he leaned against the doorjamb and watched. When they first dated, she could burn water. Now, there was a calm efficiency in every move she made and something smelled wonderful.

She glanced up at him with a wary smile. "I was bored, so I decided to make myself at home. I hope you like quiche?"

"I don't know. Never had it." He edged toward her, wondering what her reaction would be if he wrapped his arms around her waist and pulled her close to nuzzle her neck.

"What, no crack about real men not eating quiche?"

He savored the lighthearted tone in her voice. This was what he wanted—a marriage with companionship, laughter, sharing. "Real men eat whatever doesn't crawl off their plates."

"Well, at least you'll be easy to feed."

He held out her chair for her, determined to make every effort to keep their life together civil. Joining her at the table, he poked at his food, then tasted it. "This is good."

The smile almost reached her eyes. "Don't sound so surprised. If I wanted to survive, I had to learn to cook."

"Can you do meat and potatoes?"

The smile flickered over her lips again. "Don't worry, I won't let you starve."

"I wasn't worried. Cooking isn't in your job description, but I won't mind if you want to play in the kitchen."

She glared at him. "So just what do you expect me to do with myself all day?"

"Rest up for the nights."

Her fork hit the table with a sharp snap.

Knowing he was baiting her, anticipating the debate, he schooled his features into a look of bewilderment. "You can do whatever you want. Clean the house, cook the meals or sit in front of the TV all day. I don't care. There's already a housekeeper. And I can cook enough to keep myself from starving." Her mouth tightened and he waited in vain for an answer. "I told you I wouldn't be a demanding husband. What's wrong with that?"

"Far be it from me to drag you out of the Dark Ages. The little woman will find a way to amuse herself, I'm sure."

Jace scratched his jaw, secretly delighting in her reaction. "I suppose your nesting instincts are kicking in. If you want to play housewife, I don't mind."

"Jace." Her teeth were clenched, her eyes sparkling with anger. "I think it would be best if you quit while you're ahead."

This is what he'd missed. He'd forgotten just how much he enjoyed a simple argument with Danielle. And once that was over, there was the best part—the making up.

After long minutes of silence, her next words caused him to choke.

"What's to prevent me from divorcing you after I get the money?"

When the fit of coughing passed, he gulped at his coffee. "You won't."

"I could."

"Not if you want *Daddy's* business to survive."

The threat hit its target. Jace regretted the tactic but knew it was necessary.

"So you want to spend the rest of your life with a woman who doesn't love you?"

He smiled, not the least threatened by her words. "We've always gotten along. And I think you'll learn to love me."

She picked up her fork again and stabbed at her lunch. "Your arrogance boggles the mind."

He ignored her comment.

But she wasn't finished with the discussion yet. "And will you learn to love me?"

He had to admire her courage. "I tried that. Once. It was enough for me."

The hurt echoed through her green eyes, making him want to call the words back. They would both have to forget the past if they wanted any kind of a future.

"The roads should be cleared soon. I called and the snowplows are working this way." He paused. "Plan to be ready to leave in the morning."

"Leave?" Something flickered in her eyes.

A stab of regret knifed through him when he realized she was afraid. "Danielle, I'm not a monster. I have no intention of making our life together a battleground." He paused, letting those words soak in. "I hope we can learn to be friends, to enjoy each other's company. Can we at least make an effort?"

When she nodded a hesitant agreement, he cupped her cheek with his hand. "I want to start this marriage off right. We'll have a nice wedding, a short honeymoon, then I need to get back to work. Later, we'll plan a trip somewhere special.''

She gulped. ''A honeymoon isn't necessary right now. Let's just wait until you have more time.''

He cocked one eyebrow at the note of panic in her voice. ''We *will* have a honeymoon. And we *will* enjoy every moment of it.''

''So you have it all planned.'' Her lips tightened. ''And where will this wonderful honeymoon take place? Am I allowed to at least know that?''

''We'll stay at the Teton Lodge.''

Her soft gasp pleased him. She remembered. That was where he'd taken her the first time they made love. He'd wanted it to be a special memory for her. Little had he realized at the time how it would haunt him.

''But we'll have a little bigger room this time.'' He'd been on a tight budget eleven years ago. Now, he could afford whatever he wanted.

Some of the tension seemed to melt from her body. ''How long will we stay?''

''I have to be back Friday morning. And I believe you have a rather large check to deposit.''

The wonder quickly faded from her eyes at the reminder of the reason for their marriage.

''This is awkward, Jace.''

''I don't know why. I've seen you naked before, heard you purr in my arms.''

''That wasn't what I meant.''

He shrugged.

''I loved you then.'' Her voice broke and she turned away from him, but not before he saw the tears shimmering in her eyes.

He covered her hand with his, trying to offer her

some comfort. "People have successful marriages without love."

She stared at their clasped hands, his dark and tanned against hers soft and white. He was very aware of the loss of her warmth when she stood and grabbed their plates.

As she moved gracefully around the kitchen, he indulged himself. Danielle's movements always resembled a slow dance—a sexy, mind-numbing dance that never failed to turn him on.

When she set his refilled coffee cup in front of him, he caught her wrist. A gentle tug had her falling into his lap and he wrapped his arms around her, burying his nose in her fragrant hair.

"You smell the same. Even feel the same. Do you still love the same?" He nuzzled the side of her neck, anxious to remember the sweet taste of her skin.

"Jace."

The single word was a plea, but he couldn't tell for what.

"Don't, please."

He sucked in a deep breath of air, a mistake since that breath was filled with Danielle. Forcing himself to look into her green eyes, he recognized the pain and trepidation. Those were the same feelings he was battling. But he would never admit it to anyone, especially a woman who wielded far too much power over him.

"We're officially engaged." He picked up her hand and caressed her fingers, pausing at the small token of their engagement. "You even have the ring to prove it."

She tried to stand, but he held her in place, savoring the feel of her soft bottom nestled against him.

"I need time." Her soft sigh caressed his cheek. "This is all a little sudden." She shifted a little, brushing her breasts against his chest. "I would appreciate it if you wouldn't touch me before the wedding."

He loosened his hold on her but didn't release her. "You're just putting off the inevitable."

"Two days ago, my life was taking a totally different path. Give me a chance to adjust, to get used to the idea of being your...wife." Her eyes widened, sliced at his conscience. "Please, Jace."

*Damn.* He had never been able to resist her when she begged so sweetly. Tamping down his raging need, he gave a curt nod. "I won't touch you until the wedding." The promise cost him dearly. "Which is Wednesday, by the way. That gives you one more day to...adjust to the idea."

"But—"

"It's not up for negotiation. One day."

A little of the tension eased from her as she realized she had a short reprieve. But it flowed back at his next words.

"I'll expect a real wedding night, Dani. You'll be in my arms until dawn." He waited for that to soak in. "So I suggest you rest up while you have the chance. Because I don't intend to be sleeping when I have you with me."

She paled, then pulled away from him. A feeling of cold washed over him and he knew he couldn't afford to lose this time. The stakes were too high. He watched her move away, angry with himself for making such a rash promise.

As she reached around him to set down the dessert dishes, her breast brushed against the back of his hand. The heat darted through him, demanding he do something about it. But he'd just made a vow. And one thing Jace Farrell didn't do was break his word.

They finished their fresh-baked brownies in silence. Jace couldn't help but wonder if he'd pushed her too far. But she had nowhere to run, nowhere to hide. Before she had a chance to escape, he would bind her to him in more ways than one.

He stared into his half-empty coffee cup, for the first time questioning his decision to make Danielle his wife. Maybe he was setting both of them up for a fall. Maybe the resulting carnage would be impossible to heal. But he wanted her in his life again. And he hated to lose.

The clock chimed the hour. When Jace glanced up, Danielle seemed mesmerized by the cat's tail. Her teeth pulled at her lower lip and Jace found himself wanting to soothe the tortured skin. But he'd promised to give her some space.

"I need to call Daddy."

Jace nodded, feeling the old stirrings of jealousy at her devotion to her father. Knowing he was flirting with disaster, he ignored that feeling, choosing instead to torment himself with the sight of her gently swaying hips as she left the room.

# Chapter Five

Danielle closed the door to Jace's office with a sigh of relief. He was too forceful and she was beginning to fear that she would lose herself after they were married. It would take every ounce of strength she'd gained over the years to maintain her identity.

She glanced at the phone, feeling guilty for putting off the dreaded call for so long.

Her father must be frantic.

But for once, he was going to have to trust her to take care of things. For once, he was going to have to relinquish control to her. Maybe when this was over, he would finally realize that she was capable of helping him. His outdated notions about working women needed to be put aside.

At the last minute, she lost her courage and simply left a cryptic message with her father's secretary. A message that was sure to drive him to distraction. Danielle didn't reveal where she was. She merely said she was staying with friends and that he shouldn't worry, she was working on the money situation. She'd wanted to add that it was simply a matter of selling her soul.

Her father wouldn't understand her reasons for marrying Jace. She wasn't totally certain she understood herself.

After setting down the phone, Danielle fingered the locket at her throat, needing warmth, reassurance—strength. Jace's touch still had the power to ignite her needs. No other man had ever affected her that way. But how could she bear to have him touch her every day as a husband touches his wife? How could she share his bed, share her body, when there was no love between them?

How could she not after she'd pledged her life to him?

All that remained of their past love was distrust, betrayal and deception. And she couldn't see anything in their future that might be potent enough to erase their history.

Children might ease the tension between them. She'd dreamed of having their children the first time she'd been with Jace. Then, it had been a distant fantasy, something for tomorrow. But three months ago, she'd celebrated her thirtieth birthday. Her childbearing years were growing shorter.

When Jace had so callously rejected her love, she had focused all her energy on her career. After graduating from college with her business degree, she'd tried to convince her father to let her come and work for him. But he'd insisted she return to Jackson to take care of the house and perform hostess duties for him. He didn't think women belonged in the corporate world, didn't think they were hard enough, tough enough.

After months of boredom and frustration, Danielle had set out to prove him wrong. Leaving the only home she'd ever known, she'd landed a good job at an investment firm in Denver and started a slow climb to one of the top positions in the company. But her father had been unimpressed. He had decided she was just going through a phase.

When his call for help had come, she'd realized it was her last chance to convince her father she would do whatever was necessary to help the family business. And possibly her last chance to fulfill her desire for her own family.

Since agreeing to a business marriage with Raymond, she'd allowed herself to dream. Those dreams had made her feel like she was being pulled between two worlds. She'd worked so long and hard to get into her father's company, to win his approval.

Taking care of a home and raising a family held a strong appeal, too, especially if she shared that life with the right man. Suddenly, she wasn't certain she was capable of walking away from either dream without feeling like she'd cheated herself. But she was afraid to pursue them both, afraid of short-changing either fantasy.

Leaning back in Jace's leather chair, she traced a pattern on the desktop. Two boys and two girls would be her ideal family. A smile crept over her face as she pictured a miniature version of Jace, stubbornly demanding his way. There would be squabbles, but also loads of laughter, something that had been lacking in her own childhood.

On a day like today, the children would be out-side, building elaborate snow creations. Jace would be working in his office. And Danielle would be in the kitchen, baking some delectable treat for an af-ternoon snack. The warmth of her illusion washed away her apprehension for a few seconds. At the sound of Jace's voice, the negative emotions flooded back.

"Share your thoughts?"

Jace's appearance was a cold dose of reality.

The warm, cozy life she had envisioned might never exist. Unless she and Jace came to some sort of peace, their lives would never be that simple. She looked up and studied him leaning against the door frame in a deceptively casual pose. She couldn't resist the question hovering on her lips. "Do you still want to have children?"

His blue eyes darkened, his eyelids dropping slightly. "Yes." His voice was husky with an un-named emotion, that one word seeming to caress her skin.

"We used to talk about it." She glanced down at the desk, watched her finger trace the blotter. "I've always wanted four."

Pushing away from the wall, he crossed the room and perched on the edge of the desk, his jeans pull-ing taut against his hard-muscled thighs. "That's a nice round number. But I like six better."

A tingle of anticipation sparked through her. "You'd need a bigger house." She watched his face carefully, tracing every line with her gaze, des-perately trying to read his thoughts. "Do you think our marriage will survive that long?"

"Darlin', I have no intention of getting a divorce.

Those vows that say 'till death us do part' are what marriage is all about. Once you say the words, there'll be no backing out.''

A lifetime with Jace. The thought terrified her, exhilarated her.

"But can we remain married without love?"

"I'd say we have a better chance than most. Love only complicates a marriage.''

A stab of pain pierced her heart. He'd made it plain from the beginning that he didn't love her. And she certainly didn't love him, couldn't love him, after what he'd done.

"How do you feel about a working wife?"

It was very subtle, but he tensed. "My wife won't need to work. *You* won't need to work.''

"But what if I want to work?"

"You won't have time for that. I'll keep you plenty busy.''

She leaned forward in the chair, slowly starting to understand how a caged animal felt. "So after the wedding, I'll have no life of my own?"

Jace gave a low growl of frustration. "I don't want you working full-time. You'd come home exhausted every night, thinking about work. I'd have to worry about you driving into Jackson every day, rain or shine.''

"Your concern is touching. But for some reason, I don't think you're motivated by any worries for me.''

"Danielle." His voice was flat with enforced patience. "I take care of what's mine. After we're married, you'll be mine. And I won't see you hurt in any way.''

He'd take care of her physical needs masterfully,

but what about her emotional needs? "I can't just rattle around the house all day."

"I always need help. You can do the paperwork for the ranch or something." Hesitating, he seemed to be considering his words carefully. "Besides, once we have children, I hope you'll want to stay home to take care of them."

A surge of heat washed over her. Jace's children. *Their* children. "Fine. I'll work until we have children. But I won't sit around and twiddle my thumbs all day waiting for you to finish your work."

"Then I'll just have to make certain you get pregnant right away."

The words hovered between them.

Danielle stared at the desk and struggled with her emotions. He was moving too fast, binding her to him too thoroughly. The moment she said, "I do," she would never escape him.

"Are you using birth control now?"

Danielle struggled to control the heat flushing her cheeks. "There hasn't been a need."

"No boyfriends back in Denver?"

The heat flared to anger. "Well, yes. As a matter of fact, I have three waiting for me to return. I told them I needed a few weeks to settle the wedding details, then we could go back to our wild parties."

"Sarcasm doesn't suit you, Dani."

He leaned across the desk, stroked a finger down her cheek and traced a path to the neckline of her sweater. He caught the gold chain, straightening it.

"Don't use any protection after the wedding. Let's allow nature to take its course."

She couldn't seem to draw a breath. His finger teased the base of her neck.

They'd talked of the honeymoon, he'd tempted her with thoughts of sleeping together, of sharing their bodies. But putting that sharing in the context of producing a child added a whole new depth to her feelings.

Warmth pooled deep in her stomach and she couldn't help but wonder how it would feel to have a child growing there. Involuntarily, she placed a hand over her womb, an age-old, protective gesture.

His hand joined hers. "Our child, Danielle. A little spitfire with your eyes." His voice dropped to a sexy growl. "I can't wait to see you pregnant, to watch the changes in your body. And I can't wait to hold our baby." He watched her, his blue eyes intent. "You'd look beautiful with our baby nursing at your breast."

A mass of confused emotions flowed through her. His words made her feel loved, special, needed. And she wanted him, wanted him to love her. But she was so afraid her heart would get involved. If that happened, she would be handing him the ability to destroy her. Yet his words and actions made her feel like he truly loved her.

Confusion pulled at her, tangled her thoughts. Otherwise, she'd never have had the courage to ask him about the past. "Jace, what happened between us? What went so wrong?"

He stiffened, gathered the warmth he was radiating toward her and sealed himself off from her again. "I believe your father told you the entire story. I don't need to tell it again."

"I'd like to hear your side."

He didn't answer.

"Jace, I wanted to believe in you."

His jaw tightened. "What happened to trust? When a man and a woman plan to get married, they have to share a certain level of trust."

She cringed at his bitter tone, the old doubts rising to the surface again. "I didn't want to doubt you. But my father had proof."

"And it never occurred to you to ask me about my side of things?"

Her guilt blossomed. "I tried to call. You wouldn't answer your phone."

"You didn't try hard enough."

"So I was supposed to chase you all over Wyoming, begging you for answers?" Her laugh was cold, bitter. "I don't think so."

"Besides, *Daddy* is always right, isn't he?"

"Don't drag my father into this. He's a good man."

"Ah, yes. The paragon. The perfect father, the perfect businessman. Life has just handed him a raw deal and he needs to sell off his precious daughter to survive."

Danielle jumped up and slammed her hands on the desktop. "Don't talk about my father that way."

The muscles in his jaw knotted.

"My father has always been there for me. It's time for me to pay him back. And I don't mind making the sacrifice."

"I'm so glad to know that my bride-to-be is such a martyr. And how convenient that you won't require my love."

"Any chance I had of falling in love was destroyed eleven years ago."

"By your father."

"No, Jace. By you."

Tension pulsed between them.

The phone rang, shattering the strain in the room. Jace grabbed the receiver and barked out a greeting. His focus shifted and she could almost feel him pulling away from her.

"I'll be right there." The receiver landed in the cradle and Jace stood. Just when she thought he'd leave without a word, he turned. "One of my men has been hurt. I need to find a way to get him to the hospital. If we have to, we'll take him to the road on a snowmobile."

"You can't go out in this weather. It's too dangerous."

"Careful, Dani girl. Someone might think you care."

He leaned in for a quick, hard kiss, then stalked out the door.

Danielle followed him through the kitchen, pulling the curtain aside to watch him struggle through the deep snow. His sheepskin coat made his shoulders look broader than usual and she wondered if they were really strong enough to carry the weight of everyone's problems. Jace had always been completely self-contained, never seeming to need anyone else.

Including her.

When he returned, she would ask him again. She'd never heard his explanation of why he'd taken the money from her father. She'd been hurt too badly to ask questions. Being the daughter of a wealthy man all her life, she knew all too well how the game was played. The family fortune had haunted her through her teenage years.

But she'd believed Jace was different. Yes, all those years ago, he had needed money, desperately. They'd plotted and schemed on ways to save the ranch. But they'd been determined to do it together, without her father's help.

She could still remember the day it all fell apart. The pain of betrayal was as sharp now as ever. Dropping the curtain, Danielle warmed herself a cup of coffee, hoping to chase away the chill shadowing her heart.

She'd been at a fund-raising luncheon, had come home for a quick change of clothing, rushing to make an afternoon meeting. As she drove up, Jace's pickup was just leaving, turning the corner at the end of their block.

She'd never had premonitions before or since. But she had one then. She'd known something was terribly wrong. And her heart had started weeping before she'd even entered the house.

Her father had been waiting for her, all solicitous sympathy. He'd led her into his study, sat her down and held her hands. Then he'd quietly explained that Jace had accepted a large check in return for leaving Danielle alone.

It had been a test of Jace's love, her father explained. He didn't want his little girl to be hurt, so he had to be certain the man really loved her, not her money. But when Jace gladly accepted the check, Danielle's father had all the proof he needed.

She didn't want to believe her first love could betray her like that, but her father had the check carbon—and Jace's signature was at the bottom.

Her love had been worth only fifty thousand dollars.

And suddenly, horribly, certain things made sense.

Jace had never told her he loved her. Even though she said the words often, he just smiled and used her declaration as an excuse to make love. Of course, they'd used everything as an excuse to make love.

But she'd known she would never feel his hands on her skin again. He'd betrayed her heart, abused her love. And she couldn't forgive that.

Gently, Danielle's father urged his daughter to leave the area for a while. Numb with grief, Danielle had let him lead her upstairs where a maid was called to pack her bags. The sun hadn't even settled in the horizon before Danielle was on her way to Denver to stay with an aunt.

When Danielle finally crawled out of the emotional hole she'd dug, she realized she'd have to make a new life for herself. First, she'd asked to join her father in the business. He'd hedged, said she wasn't qualified. So she'd enrolled in college and worked hard to earn her degree in business. Again, her father refused her help, saying she didn't have the experience.

Determined to prove herself to him and to the rest of the world, she found a job in Denver and proceeded to work her way up the corporate ladder. If she couldn't have the marriage and family she'd always wanted, she would find satisfaction in her work. And she'd actually managed to convince herself she was happy, spending little time analyzing her life.

Then her father had called, all but begging for

her help. And Danielle had realized just how cold and lonely she truly was.

But now, she had to wonder. With Jace gone, something vital had left the house. Once again, she was alone, with only the sound of the mournful wind to keep her company. There was a huge danger in allowing him to be that important in her life.

Danielle spent the afternoon prowling the house, lost in doubts and memories. Only time would tell if she was doing the right thing. She couldn't see any other choice. To let her father lose the business would kill him. He was the only constant in her life, the one person who had always been there to help her pick up the pieces.

She lightly touched the necklace at her throat. The debt she owed him might never be repaid. He'd been her rock for too long for her to turn her back on him now.

When she heard the door open again, darkness had settled over the ranch. Jace shook off a shower of snow and shut out the night. With a tired sigh, he leaned against the frame, watching her through half-closed eyes, his hat shadowing his expression. Then he pulled off his gloves, his gaze never wavering. "I could get used to this."

Nerves fluttered through her when she reminded herself that she would ask him about that fateful day—tonight.

She offered Jace a slight smile, desperately needing to make an effort to lighten the mood between them. "Aren't you supposed to say, 'Hi, honey, I'm home,' or something like that?"

He pushed away from the door and unbuttoned

his coat. "Hi, honey, I'm home." He waited. "Don't I get a kiss?"

She licked her lips, wanting his touch more than she was willing to admit. Shrugging her doubts aside, she crossed to him. An icy chill radiated from him and she shivered when she placed her hands on his chest. Stretching upward, she pressed her mouth against his cold lips.

"Is everything okay?" The question sounded forced, but it helped her feel like there was hope for their future.

As the afternoon had dragged toward the end, she'd made a private vow to be a good wife, no matter what. If Jace would meet her halfway, they could share a satisfying life.

His arms closed around her, crushing her against his length. He tipped his head to avoid hitting her with his hat brim, then ravaged her mouth. "A lot better now."

Danielle struggled to regain her equilibrium. Once again, he'd swamped her senses, made her lose all notion of right and wrong. Even the cold from his clothing couldn't quell the heat he'd ignited deep inside her.

She forced herself to step away. "Is your hired hand okay?"

Jace nodded as he hung up his coat. "We got him to the ambulance and I checked on him before I came in. He'll be fine."

She struggled for more words to fill the room. "I've already eaten. Can I fix you something?"

He shook his head. "I ate with the guys in the bunkhouse. I figured you'd be tired."

*Start off as you intend to proceed.* The words

echoed through her mind. She refused to spend every evening by herself, only sharing his company as he chose to dole it out. "I hope you don't plan to make a habit of that." She winced inwardly. Her voice sounded waspish, complaining.

He caught her arm as she started to turn away. Reeling her in slowly, he tugged her closer, so close the snow from his boots puddled onto her nylon-clad feet.

When his mouth was just inches away from hers, he spoke. "I don't. I just didn't want to impose on you tonight. There'll be time enough for us to settle into a routine. A lifetime." He sealed that promise with a soft touch of his mouth to hers.

Her heart melted, puddling like the water on the floor, and she leaned closer, wanting, needing, more.

"Come sit by the fire with me."

She could only nod her agreement.

"Some hot coffee would taste good. Make some?"

Again, she nodded.

Her hands shook as she struggled to measure out the coffee grounds. After spilling half of them on the countertop, she set down the measure and inhaled deeply.

All right, she would admit it. She was scared, terrified. The past few minutes had shown her how wonderful their marriage could be. What she was about to ask Jace could change everything, for better or for worse.

Danielle didn't know which terrified her more.

If things worsened between them, her marriage would be a living torment. If their relationship improved, she would give her heart to him again. Only Jace held the ability to destroy her love—and her along with it.

A gentle hand settled on her shoulder, another one covered her hand resting beside the coffee measure. "Are you okay?"

Not wanting him to question her further, she forced her eyes open, willing herself to concentrate, and glued a smile to her lips. "I'm fine. You were right. I am tired. Must be the weather." He stood nearby as she finished her task. When the coffeemaker was gurgling, she urged him from the kitchen. "Why don't you start a fire, get warm, and I'll bring the coffee in a minute."

He stared at her, hard, then turned and walked away.

She begged silently for the strength to hide her fears from him. They couldn't go on until they'd resolved the past. Deep in her heart, she knew that. But it was tempting to simply sweep it under the rug and try to forget about it.

She laughed softly. She'd been trying to forget for over a decade. And now, she had a daily reminder sharing the house with her. It would be impossible to overlook their shared history under those conditions.

She poured the coffee and followed Jace. He was hunched in front of the fireplace, feeding kindling into the flames. As she handed him one mug, their fingers brushed. Silently, she pleaded for his understanding. Nerves stretched taut, she retreated to the couch and curled up, snagging a pillow to cuddle.

When he glanced over his shoulder, he looked at the pillow, then met her gaze, a question in his eyes.

She looked away rather than try to explain how alone she felt. The fire snapped, pulling her from her thoughts. She would've liked to ease into the discussion, bring it gently around to the painful part, but she didn't know how.

"Tell me, Jace. What really happened that day with my father?"

This time, he didn't stiffen. He stared into the fledgling flames and she wondered if he'd answer her at all.

Finally, he spoke. "What does it matter? You made your decision years ago. I doubt anything I have to say now will change that."

He wasn't going to make this easy. "I wanted to believe in you so badly."

"Apparently not badly enough."

Her heart twisted. "I loved you."

"But you didn't believe in me."

Those words stabbed her conscience. She'd tried so hard, but the evidence had been overwhelming.

The wind moaned outside, reminding her just how cold she felt inside. Clutching the coffee mug, she tried to absorb its warmth. "You never once said you loved me."

He snapped a stick in half and fed it to the flames. "Words have never been important to me."

"They were to me. I needed to hear them."

"Are you fishing to hear them now?"

She didn't, couldn't, answer. Emotions filled her throat, making words impossible.

"You won't. I'll never give my love to a woman. All women are interested in is money and power."

She gasped in disbelief. "You can't believe I was after your money then."

He laughed, but the sound held no amusement. "No, I can't. I didn't have any. Maybe that was the attraction. I was the forbidden, the unknown. The poor boy from the other side of town." The sharp snap of another stick emphasized his words. "I was a novelty, wasn't I? It was all a game to you."

She tried to tamp the anger down. "I don't play those kinds of games."

"So what was it, Dani? Why me?"

"I told you. I loved you." To her humiliation, her voice trembled.

"That's not what your father said."

Danielle bit her lip, confusion making it impossible to think. "Why did you ask him for the money?"

"He offered it." Jace's words were short, clipped.

Her world tilted, all her beliefs sliding into a jumbled mass she was certain she would never get sorted out. "Why?"

"How the hell should I know?" His shoulders lifted as he pulled air into his lungs. His next words were softer, but the anger still loomed in his voice. "He told me he wanted you to be happy and he knew this would give me a chance to get the ranch settled."

She waited, wanting to believe, but not daring to allow herself. Her father would never lie to her.

"I didn't want the money. I wanted to do it by myself. But your father doesn't take no for an answer. Finally, I agreed to take the money as a loan. With interest." Jace dragged a hand through his hair but didn't turn to face her. "Danielle, he didn't tell you the truth that day."

"Daddy wouldn't do that."

Jace let his silence answer her.

Her heart shattered and she felt that all her hopes for her future with Jace had been dashed. If he couldn't be honest with her now, they stood little chance of having a real relationship. "Are you calling my father a liar?"

"That seems like a harsh word. I do know when I went to the bank, payment had been stopped on the check. And when I called your house, you were gone."

The tension stretched between them until Danielle was certain something would snap.

A low rumble sounded in the distance. Jace stood, effectively breaking the standoff. He pulled the window shade aside. "Finally. Snowplows."

Still clutching the pillow, Danielle rose to her feet. With a flood of relief, she realized she could escape. She needed to get away from the magnetism he radiated. She needed time to think, to regroup.

"I want to go home, Jace. I'll call you in the morning." As she tried to move past him, he caught her arm, halting her retreat.

"You are home, Danielle."

# Chapter Six

The light of battle faded from her eyes, filling Jace with regrets. But he couldn't let her go now.

Not when he was so close to having her again.

"Then I'll go to bed." Shaking off his hand, she turned and left the room, taking with her the goodnight kiss he'd been hoping for.

Alone in the room, Jace thought back on the past eleven years.

The old man had failed.

Years ago, Jace's father had spirited away a prime piece of ranch land from the Simmons family. Danielle's father had been embarrassed and humiliated by the loss and didn't forgive easily.

Tyrone Simmons had not only wanted to keep Danielle away from a man he considered unfit for his daughter, but he'd wanted to destroy the son of a man who'd dared to defy the power of the Simmons family. Jace had finally managed to outmaneuver Simmons on both counts.

So why did Jace have the sense he was teetering on the edge of failure?

Trying to rub the exhaustion from the back of his neck, he stared into the fire. Because Danielle might never learn to love him again. Their past stood between them, muddying the waters of their future. In spite of all the lies between them, he wanted to bask in the warmth her love would offer.

And maybe, just maybe, he would allow his heart to feel something for her, even if he wouldn't let himself fall in love with her again. He couldn't forgive her for her lack of faith all those years ago. But they could learn to go on, find a way to make a satisfying life.

To start with, they had the passion that burned between them, a passion that had never faded. Surely that was enough to sustain a marriage.

He could only hope for the best.

Closing the glass doors to the fireplace, he glanced at the empty stairway with regret. All afternoon, while he'd fought the cold and the snow, he'd thought of Danielle, of sharing a pleasant evening with her in front of this very fire.

How long would it take before they learned to be friends?

Maybe he hadn't won yet. Simmons was still a big influence in Danielle's life. And she might never believe what her father was capable of.

But once she lived in this house every day, once her father became a more distant figure in her life, then Jace was hopeful he stood a chance.

He surveyed the empty room. There would be no sleep for him again tonight. Danielle taunted him even when she was closeted away in another room.

Wearily, he went to his office and closed the door. The nice thing about a ranch the size of his was that the work was never finished.

The lone suitcase sat at the back door. Jace's truck was warmed and waiting, a path to the main road plowed clear. He was dressed and ready for their wedding in a charcoal-gray Western-cut suit.

All he needed now was Danielle.

And he needed her so desperately it scared him. He'd lost her before and barely survived. If he allowed his heart to feel a second time, he didn't think he could bear to lose her. So he chose to seal up his emotions and keep her at a distance. Besides, until she could show that she trusted him, believed in him, he needed to hold her at arm's length.

The floor creaked, announcing her arrival in the kitchen, and all his vows evaporated.

Still wearing the same outfit on day three, she looked amazingly well groomed. But the dark smudges under her eyes attested to the fact that she had again slept little more than he had.

She flashed him a wan smile and held up her purse and coat. "I guess I'm all packed."

"I thought we'd have breakfast on the road, then try to do some shopping before we leave town." He glanced at his watch. "The minister won't be available until three o'clock, so we should have plenty of time to get everything you need."

A tremor of reaction shook her delicate frame and she edged back one step. "I'm not really hungry."

Wanting to hold her, comfort her, he forced himself to remain where he was, not certain of his reception. Crossing his arms, he made a silent plea for the right words, for her understanding.

"I'd like to get along, Danielle. Why make both our lives miserable by constantly fighting?"

Mimicking his posture, she crossed her arms and leaned against the opposite wall. "You'll have everything you want after we're married."

He didn't dare admit her words were true.

"So what's in it for me?" she asked.

He couldn't resist, even offered her a tentative smile. "Me?"

She shook her head. "Not good enough. You've slandered my family, threatened me, forced me to marry you. I repeat, what's in it for me?"

"That sounds like a bad melodrama." When the anger flashed in her eyes, he raised a hand to forestall her angry words. "I apologize. That was uncalled for."

She didn't respond.

"Would it be enough to offer you security, the family you want and enough loving to chase away the coldest night?"

Her anger softened and he knew he'd won a temporary victory.

"Can we agree to disagree over the past?" He waited for her response, but she simply watched him. "We will be married." Still, she didn't respond. "How about a truce in the meantime? We have the rest of our lives to resolve this."

After a long hesitation, she nodded, but the movement was tight, filled with her misgivings.

Unable to resist the uncertainty radiating from her, he crossed the room, then nudged her chin up until she was forced to look at him. The anguish reflected in her green eyes almost stopped his head-long pursuit. Everything would be all right. Everything *had* to be all right. He would make it right. Just as he'd made everything else in his life happen. Hard work and sheer force of will had carried him far.

"We'll be okay. I promise." His voice was a ragged whisper.

He sealed his vow with a brush of his lips against hers. His reaction was swift, hot. Tonight, she would belong to him. He would finally be able to touch her, to relearn the ways of her body.

Her sigh feathered across his cheek. "I want to believe you."

"Then do." He cupped her cheek, wanting to offer more, but knowing he needed time to show her the life they could share.

Her lips turned up slightly. "You make it sound so easy."

He wanted to kiss her again, wanted to taste the depths of her mouth. But he knew if he touched her lips now, he would make love to her right here, on the kitchen floor. The hours of darkness had been filled with images of her and he was hanging on to his control by a mere thread. He wanted better for this reunion, wanted the moment to be special.

"What's easy is for you to spend my money." He forced himself away from her but couldn't resist taking her hand. Just a touch, that was all he needed to get him through the day. If he could hold her hand, he could assure himself that the night was drawing closer and let his need build.

He was anxious to get the day started, but she resisted when he tried to urge her forward. Her chin came up in a gesture he was becoming very familiar with. "I'll buy my own clothes. I have money of my own."

He almost grinned. He enjoyed a good fight, savored a challenge. Danielle offered both in generous doses. "No, you can pick them out. Although I reserve the right of final approval. And I get to pay for it."

"Jace."

"Danielle." He mimicked her tone of voice, then softened. "Don't feel like you have to fight me on everything. As your husband, I'll expect to pay for whatever you need." He opened the door, needing the cold blast of air to focus his thoughts on the mundane act of shopping. "Besides, you forget. I can afford it."

Her eyes snapped with challenge and he knew the discussion wasn't over yet. "And you think I can't." She pulled on her coat and started for the door, pride in every step.

He rubbed his chin, hating to disrupt her graceful retreat. "Uh, Dani?"

She stopped, turned, glared at him.

"I, uh, never rescued your shoes from the mud."

She groaned.

"I'd say they're under about two feet of snow right now. Even if I could find them, they'd be ruined."

She squeezed her eyes shut and he could almost hear her count to ten. "Well, I can't very well go into town barefoot."

He grinned, finding more humor in the situation than she did. "I'd offer you a pair of mine, but I don't think they'd stay on your feet."

She glared at her toes, then looked to him. "So what do you plan to do about it?"

"Me?" He thumbed his hat brim up and stared at her in surprise.

"It's your fault." A gleam entered her green eyes and her body relaxed slightly.

He'd forgotten this side of her—the playful imp who could tease and torment with equal skill.

She nodded, her lips pursed. "You carried me inside. It was your responsibility to take care of the shoes, too."

"I see." He considered the problem for a moment, tantalized with the possibilities. "Then I guess I'll just have to carry you out." With a quick stride, he was in front of her. Before she could do more than grasp his shoulders, he cradled her in his arms.

Exactly where she belonged.

"And do you plan to carry me into all the stores?"

"Just the first one. After that, everyone in town will know you belong to me."

She bit her lip and the tension flowed back into her body.

Jace placed her on the front seat of his truck, then returned to pick up his suitcase and close the door. Anticipation curled through him. He halted, surveyed his land and allowed himself a smile. It had seemed like the impossible dream at times, but he was finally going to make all his plans happen—all *their* plans. Danielle had been a big part of weaving those fantasies so long ago. It had been her leaving that had driven him to succeed.

The drive into town was accomplished in silence.

Jace focused his attention on the freshly plowed roads, trying to give Danielle some time to adjust to this next step in their relationship.

But each time she stirred, an image sifted through his thoughts, an image from the past, of Danielle when she had still loved him. Each gentle sigh, every rustle of clothing, brought back a memory. Her soft perfume wove through his senses, distracting him from what was important—which was getting his ring on her finger and binding her to him in every way possible.

After parking in front of a large department store, Jace went around to help Danielle out. When he reached inside the truck to scoop her up, she swatted his shoulder. "I can walk. Please don't embarrass me, Jace."

He leaned back against the door, studied the puddle of slush between her and the sidewalk, then the icy concrete, covered with mud and salt. "Darlin', I don't plan on throwing down my coat for you. And I don't think your legs are long enough for that first jump."

She hesitated, her gaze following the same path. He could see the exact moment when she decided a graceful exit was impossible. "Do you always have to be right?"

"Yes, ma'am. I sure do." Before she could protest again, he swept her up. At her squeak of surprise, several pedestrians stopped and stared. Danielle tried to push away from him and he couldn't resist dropping her just a few inches. When she had her arms wrapped tightly around his neck, he started for the double glass doors.

As soon as her feet were warmly encased in sleek

snow boots, she proceeded to show him how a true professional shopped. And he didn't even get right of refusal on any of her outfits. Quick as a Wyoming blizzard, she would select several items from the rack, disappear into the dressing room and reappear with her selections. All that was left for him to do was pay the bills. A job he enjoyed almost as much.

But by the fourth store, he was becoming bored. It had never occurred to him that a woman would need so many different things. Waiting outside one more dressing room, he allowed his mind free rein.

Tonight.

Glancing at his watch, he counted the hours. He could satisfy all his desires, all his fantasies—tonight. Finally, he would sleep with her in his arms through the dark hours, waking up with the morning sun reflected on her tousled sleepiness so he could make love to her again.

No matter how hurt and angry he'd become over the years, that fantasy had never died. His need for her had never faded. It had only ripened with time until he was certain he would die for the wanting.

When she stepped out of the dressing room, he halted her with a hand on her arm. She turned, a half smile on her lips, all traces of what stood between them temporarily forgotten. This was how he wanted it to be. Every day, for the rest of their lives.

He curled his fingers into the silky hair at the nape of her neck, lightly massaging the soft skin. "Kiss me?"

He wanted her to come to him this time. He needed to know she was willing.

Her eyes took on a sly look, her lips curled upward, and she laughed, soft and deep. The sound settled in his belly, igniting a slow burn of desire.

She raised a hand, lightly scratching a fingernail across his cheek. "Only if you say please, cowboy."

"Please?" He held his breath when she inched closer, then hesitated as the blood thundered through his veins. "Pretty please?" He half expected her to pull away at the last second and laugh. But she surprised him. Shocked him, actually.

Her tongue peeked out to trace his lips and he leaned back against the wall, bracing his legs and tucking her close against his thighs. His mouth opened on a low groan and she met his tongue eagerly. Heat flooded through him and he lost all consciousness of where they were and what they had to overcome. Her fingers curled into his chest and she didn't seem inclined to end their mating any time soon.

When she finally pulled away, they were both breathing hard. He would never make it until after the wedding. "Dani, my girl, you are dangerous."

She grinned and pulled away. "Especially when I have your credit card."

"I can think of a better way to spend the afternoon than shopping."

"You said you could afford it."

"Oh, I can. But you're driving me crazy." He pushed away from the wall. "Besides, I'm not used to all this concrete. My feet are howling. Let's find a place to sit down for a while."

Needing a breather, he led her to a small café where they ordered a light lunch.

While they waited for their food, Danielle

searched through her purchases, making certain she hadn't forgotten anything. "I have to stop at the drugstore for some toiletries and I think I'm done."

He'd been with her all morning and hadn't seen her select the one thing he'd wanted most for her today. "I'd like you to pick out a wedding dress."

"That won't be necessary, Jace. I'll just wear one of my new outfits."

He raised an eyebrow. "I didn't see any dresses in those bags."

"It seems a little impractical to do the June Cleaver thing on your ranch."

"So you plan to wear pants to your own wedding?" Anger built inside him. He knew it was totally unreasonable, still he couldn't help but sense that she wasn't taking their relationship seriously. He didn't want to simply play house. He wanted to build a lifetime with her.

She winced. "I forgot. Usually when I shop, I get suits for work. One of those would be perfect. If we stop by the house, it would only take me a minute to gather everything together."

He pictured her, hair tight, clothes buttoned up, a businesslike mask on her face. That wasn't what he wanted for his bride. "No suit." Jace bent forward, determined to be reasonable, but just as determined to make her change her mind. "I want to see you walking toward me in something special, something soft. Do it for me."

Her joy from the morning faded away and she looked down. "You almost act as if we're marrying for love." She traced a fold in the pristine white tablecloth, her voice low.

He reached across the table, needing contact with

her, wanting her to understand. "Dani." He sighed when he saw the flash of irritation in her eyes. "I don't want to fight you every step of the way. But I do want you to have a nice wedding."

"That's a lovely thought, Jace, but a little out of character with the rest of your caveman tactics. Besides, I imagine we'll simply have a quick ceremony in front of the preacher and get on with our lives."

Every little girl dreamed of her wedding. Because of their circumstances, he was forced to deny her those satin-and-lace fantasies. Jace tried to ignore the guilt tweaking at his conscience. It would still be a memorable time for them. He would make it memorable. The plans had been set and he had every intention of surprising her. But now it was essential to gain her cooperation.

He nodded as a bowl of soup was placed in front of her. "Eat your lunch. We have some ground to cover in the next hour."

It took almost all of that hour before they found what Jace was looking for. The dress was a soft, flowing creation of satin and lace that showed just enough of her leg to tease and tempt.

As if she didn't already tempt him to distraction.

"Do you like it?" He held the dress up for her inspection.

"It's beautiful, Jace." She smiled softly, reaching out to finger a section of lace. "Very romantic." Then she spoiled it all by checking the price tag. "But far too expensive for something I'll only wear once."

He cocked an eyebrow. "Somehow I doubt price has ever stopped you before."

She had the grace to look a little abashed.

"Nothing's too expensive for my bride." It didn't take much encouragement for her to try it on and he insisted she model it for him.

She peeked over the dressing-room door. "But it's bad luck for you to see me in my dress before the wedding."

"Sweetness, if we haven't jinxed this wedding yet, we can't possibly do it now. Let me see you."

His heart stopped when she stepped out and shyly did a slow turn for him.

His bride. His wife.

Words he thought he'd never have an opportunity to use in connection with Danielle. He frowned when he caught the gleam of the locket she never seemed to be without. But when she stepped closer and peered at him through her eyelashes, he forgot all about the ever present piece of jewelry.

"Do you like it?"

Stroking his fingers across her cheek, he lowered his head to tease her lips with his own. "You are beautiful." His mouth sought hers again. He kept the kiss chaste and sweet, pride for his bride-to-be swelling inside him. "Wear the dress to the lodge. Let me enjoy you in it until the ceremony."

She nodded her agreement.

The clerk quickly picked out accessories, helped remove the tags and rang up the purchases. Jace experienced a twinge of regret when she covered the dress with her long wool coat but consoled himself with the thought of revealing the dress later, when the moment was perfect.

As they walked by the lingerie department, Jace couldn't resist pausing to finger a see-through creation designed with the express purpose of driving a man wild. His imagination filled in the flowing material and he could envision Danielle, waiting for him, a welcoming light in her eyes.

"No, Jace."

Her tone was laced with amusement but brooked no argument.

He turned and almost grinned at the high spots of color in her cheeks. She knew exactly what he'd been thinking. "Why not? It would be perfect for our wedding night."

"I thought this was a business merger."

"Does that mean we can't enjoy ourselves?"

"Yes." She went over to another rack, one with serviceable flannel nightgowns on sale. Winnowing through the choices, she finally held one up. "What do you think of this?"

The high collar and long sleeves left everything to the imagination, and the frolicking teddy bears printed on the fabric were anything but sexy. But Jace figured the gown would keep her warm when he wasn't available to do the job himself. "I'd say it's perfect." He smiled when she blinked at him in surprise. Two could play this game. A game he fully intended to win.

Suddenly impatient to get on the road, Jace paid for the nightgown and hustled Danielle outside. They had one more stop to make, the most important one of all.

When he parked in front of the courthouse, Danielle stared at the building for a long moment. Jace walked around to her door, pulled it open and held out his hand.

"Should I carry you inside?"

She stiffened before a smile tugged at her lips. "That would certainly give them something to talk about." She stepped down without his help, but when she tried to walk past him, he grabbed her hand, tucking her fingers into his.

The paperwork was short, impersonal. Then the clerk spoiled her stern image with a smile and a wink. "Have fun, kids."

It was a matter of minutes until they were on the outskirts of Jackson, headed for the lodge—and their destiny.

Laboring snowplows left them idling on the highway for almost thirty minutes. With each second that ticked by, Jace felt his impatience build. He checked his watch, figured they still had plenty of time and tried not to anticipate the evening ahead.

He would move slowly with Dani if it killed him. He wanted to indulge himself and take extra time to learn the changes eleven years had made in her body, make certain he fulfilled her every wish and desire.

But most of all, he wanted to hold her while she came apart in his arms. He wanted to watch as the need and desire grew to a breaking point in her, then push her over the edge. And he wanted to do it over and over.

When they arrived at the lodge, it was to discover that their room wasn't ready yet. The impatience simmered hotter.

"I'm sorry, sir," the manager explained. "Because of the weather, not all our staff were able to make it to work today. We're running a bit behind schedule."

Jace bit back harsh words, certain the powers-that-be were trying to test his resistance to Danielle. After securing their luggage, he turned to her, asking what she wanted to do for the next hour.

"Run away?"

The twinkle in her eyes assured him she was only partly serious. As the day wore on, she had become more comfortable with him, with their situation. The tensions between them had shifted and become tangled with a potent blend of discovery and desire.

When he didn't respond, she made another suggestion. "Let's just look around. This is such a beautiful area and I want to catch a little sun before it goes back into hibernation again."

They wandered the carefully shoveled pathway that led through a snow-covered garden. Jace smiled when he realized he was trying to think of excuses to take her hand in his. He'd cupped her elbow to help her over several icy patches, but she'd immediately pulled away again. He wanted a connection with her, an assurance.

Finally, he realized he didn't need a reason. And with a firm grasp, he pulled her hand into his and laced their fingers together. She glanced at him, obviously puzzled, but didn't try to pull away.

Their silence was comfortable, companionable until she spoke again. "Do you really believe my father set you up?"

A different kind of tension flowed through him. Stopping, Jace stared at the Grand Tetons in the distance, hoping to draw strength from the craggy peaks. He couldn't tell her, not yet, not while their relationship was still so fragile.

But one day she would have to know that two years after she'd left town, her father had gloated at a party about how he'd gotten rid of that worthless Jace Farrell. And when Jace walked into that conversation, everyone else had shown the good sense to melt away.

But Tyrone Simmons had smiled at Jace and announced that finally they were even. Jace's father had outmaneuvered the Simmons company in a land deal years before Jace was even born. The failed deal had cost the wealthy family both in money and in pride.

In Tyrone's mind, he had not only rescued his precious daughter from a poverty-stricken existence, but he'd also extracted a belated revenge in the process. Everything had worked out perfectly for the Simmons family once again.

And Jace knew he couldn't admit that he'd gone to her engagement party to prove Simmons was the true loser. Jace wanted to show the family that he'd succeeded without their help and was now more successful than they were. He wanted to rub their noses in the fact that if he chose to, he could save them. But he'd had no intention of offering.

Then he'd seen Danielle for the first time in too many years and some unnamed emotion had kicked him in the gut. His motives and intentions shifted. He'd remembered what had brewed between them before.

And he wanted it again.

Today, she was almost within his grasp.

Danielle touched his arm, bringing his attention back to her, to the moment. "I need an answer, Jace. Do you really believe my father set you up?"

He sighed, not wanting to ruin their tenuous truce

with the truth. He tugged his hat a little lower over his eyes. "Yes, I do."

Pain and doubt flickered over her features. "Why?"

"Maybe someday I'll tell you." He glanced at his watch, relieved to see they needed to meet with the minister soon. "Right now, I believe we have a wedding to attend."

A frown marred her smooth forehead. "I believe I'd like you to answer me now." The quiet insistence in her voice gave him pause.

If he said anything, an argument would ensue. And she could get angry enough to refuse to go through with her promise.

Glad of the interruption, he watched as a clerk from the lodge made his way toward them.

"Your room will be ready in about an hour."

Jace held back his growing frustration. This wasn't anyone's fault, unless he wanted to get angry at the weather.

"I'm afraid I have some additional bad news."

One more delay and Jace was certain he'd lose his temper. As it was, his demand was sharp. "What?"

"The minister has been delayed. Due to the heavy snow, he won't arrive until morning. He promised to try to be here by nine o'clock."

The fantasies of the night ahead disappeared in a puff of reality. And the desire that had been intensifying all day clenched at his insides.

Danielle's quiet sigh of relief only irritated Jace further.

# Chapter Seven

The walk to their room was a tension-filled, silent affair. When they stopped in front of the door, Danielle turned to face him, tempted to hold out her hand for a handshake in order to set the tone for their goodbye.

But she didn't.

Because she realized that she really wanted him to kiss her. But if she allowed that, she wouldn't have the strength to halt what might develop.

He took a step toward her.

She retreated against the door, trying to resolve her inner battle.

His eyes spoke of seduction. "We'll be married in the morning."

Danielle clenched her hands into fists to prevent herself from pulling him closer, to keep herself from weaving her fingers through his thick hair. Dipping his head, Jace nibbled a path of kisses from her chin to the neckline of her wedding dress.

He tempted her so badly.

"Jace, please."

He paused, sucked in a deep breath and raised his gaze to meet hers. The blue fire burning in his eyes almost made her relent. She wanted those flames to consume her, to burn away the pain of their past.

"I want you, Danielle. And I'm not willing to wait another night to have you."

It took all her willpower to push her hands against his chest. He inched back just enough to give her room to breathe, but not enough so she could think clearly. With one hand braced against the door behind her, he watched, waited. All she had to cling to was her vow not to make love with him until they were married. It had been a meaningful promise when she'd made it, even if that importance was fading in the face of his desire.

She slid away from him, away from temptation. He remained as he was, his back to her.

"You're going to refuse me again?"

"I'll be your wife in every way after the wedding. Please respect that, respect me."

He finally turned to face her. "Oh, I respect you." His grin was a rueful twist of his lips. "That doesn't make me want you any less." Reluctance in every move, he crossed the hall to the second room he'd been obliged to rent. "And that won't make my bed any warmer tonight." He unlocked the door, then turned to face her once more. "Are you sure?"

She wasn't. But she couldn't back down now. "Yes." The word was barely loud enough for her to hear, but he understood and nodded before disappearing into his room.

Danielle stood in the empty hallway, listening to the rapid staccato of her own heart, willing her breathing to slow. After a moment, she opened her own door, closing it with a decisive click.

A mirror image of herself waited inside and Danielle studied her reflection ruefully. All dressed up and no place to go.

Frustration filled her.

She'd been granted a short reprieve. But suddenly, she wasn't completely certain she wanted it.

The day with Jace had been close to perfect. Their hours together had reminded her why she had fallen in love with him the first time. The marriage was inevitable. And so was the loving.

She wanted the ceremony over with, the vows spoken and witnessed. She wanted to spend the night in Jace's arms, wanted to remember how safe and secure she'd always felt with him in the past. She wanted to melt the cold ice that had settled around her heart.

Danielle looked around the cozy room with regret. It was a room for lovers. The fireplace had been lit by a well-trained bellhop and glowed with a friendly flame. The lights were turned low and every piece of furniture had been selected with the comfort of two lovers in mind. A bottle of champagne was chilling by the bed.

Not even the teasing bubbles of the numbing wine would keep her warm tonight.

She trailed her fingers across the downy quilt. It seemed a waste to sleep alone in the big four-poster bed. But one of the few things left in her life that she still had control over was when she and Jace made love. And she intended to make him wait until they were married, even if it killed her.

Stretching and straining, she managed to tug down the zipper at the back of her wedding dress. For a moment, she toyed with the idea of walking across the hall and asking Jace for his help. But she also knew exactly where that would lead. Her actions would be an open invitation.

Pulling off her dress, she carefully hung it in the closet, smoothing her hand over the white lace. It was a lovely dress and it warmed her heart to think that Jace cared enough to pick it out for her.

As she slid her new nightgown over her head, she knew even the soft flannel wouldn't manage to warm her tonight. And she wished that she had let Jace buy her the frothy creation he'd been fingering.

She wanted him so badly she ached with the need.

As she slipped between the cool sheets, she couldn't halt memories of Jace's touch, his kisses. Punching her pillow, she berated herself for her own stubbornness. It was going to be a long night.

But to her surprise, she slept straight through until a knock at her door roused her from a deep sleep. Waking slowly, she found her arms wrapped around the extra pillow as if she were embracing her lover. She shrank away from the image, uncomfortable with how often her thoughts were occupied with the idea of making love to Jace.

The knock sounded again.

Shoving a tangle of curls from her eyes, she stumbled to the door, cringing as the cool air swept up her nightgown. Without questioning her early morning caller, she jerked the door open.

And forgot how to breathe at the sight of a handsome cowboy draped against the door frame, his arms crossed, his smile slowly fading.

"You're beautiful even in flannel." Jace's voice held a husky throb. Without hesitation, he reached for her and drew her close. As her unrestrained breasts came into contact with the hard plane of his chest, desire swamped her. Her blood awoke and hummed through her veins, wiping away all traces of sleepiness.

His mouth covered hers, his tongue begging entry—a request she gladly granted. His hands cupped her bottom and pulled her more tightly to him, wedging her against the evidence of his own burgeoning desire. She wanted to invite him in, to let nature take its course, but this time, it was Jace who resisted temptation.

He drew in a ragged breath. "I came to see if you wanted breakfast." A grin flashed over his lips as a wicked wink closed one eye. "I wasn't expecting you to be the main course."

A few more hours. She just had to resist that deadly charm a few more hours. Then she could share the lovemaking without feeling as if she'd lost a major battle. Confident in her ability to control the situation, she smiled and leaned back to study his face.

"I'm not on the menu. But if you'll give me thirty minutes, I'll be ready to join you downstairs."

He sighed in exaggerated disappointment. "I guess I could settle for bacon and eggs."

She pushed the door closed on his wounded expression, feeling a tingle of anticipation—a tingle that stayed with her until she opened the door again. Her breath caught when she saw Jace, still leaning against the doorjamb, desire smoldering in his gaze.

"I, uh, thought you were going downstairs."

"I wanted to go with you."

His words filled her with warmth. Was it possible for them to overlook the past? Fear nibbled at her joy. They had to learn to trust each other again. But Danielle was even more afraid of what would follow. Because if she allowed herself to trust, love would surely be the final result. And only Jace held the ability to destroy her. In all the years they were apart, she'd never met another man who held such power over her emotions. She'd barely survived the first time Jace had turned away from her. A second time would be a mortal wound.

She looked into the burning eyes of her fiancé. This was her wedding day. Danielle forcefully swept her doubts aside. She would enjoy the moment, savor Jace's attentions. The past would still be with them another time. But for now, she wanted happy memories to cling to just in case their past did catch up with them.

After a light breakfast, Jace went to the front desk to check on the status of their snowbound minister.

"No sign of him yet." Jace took her hand, an action that had seemed foreign yesterday, but today was natural, right. She threaded her fingers through his, savoring the strength he offered.

"So what do we do until he arrives?"

Jace's answer was in his eyes.

"No."

"Are you a mind reader?"

"I don't have to be. You've made it very clear these past few days just what your short-term goals are."

He moved closer, tucking her into the circle of his arms. "And how do you know my long-term goals aren't the same?"

She could learn to subsist on his passion alone. It fed an empty place in her heart that she hadn't managed to fill in the corporate world.

He suggested another walk outside and she agreed, thinking the fresh air would clear her mind, help release the sensual hold Jace seemed to have woven around her. It was becoming more and more difficult to view their relationship rationally, to remember that their marriage was a business arrangement, not a love match.

But when they walked to the glassed front of the lodge, a cold wind was swirling the snow while heavy clouds covered the jewel-blue sky of yesterday. Not a bad omen, she hoped. With the ragged mountain peaks in the distance, the scene looked frosty and foreboding.

A shiver raced through her, but the chill immediately turned to warmth when Jace draped an arm across her shoulders.

"Cold?"

She smiled and shook her head, not willing to admit to the negative bent of her thoughts.

"Let's browse through the gift shop. Maybe I'll find a wedding present for you."

"You don't need to buy me anything." He'd

given her too much already and her pride felt the sting.

"I want to. I want to give you something special to remember this day."

*I'll have you.* The words almost slipped from her lips. But she couldn't bear to shatter the fragile truce growing between them with any reminders of what waited for them back in Jackson.

They wandered among the displays, stopping to examine various pieces of Western-flavored artwork. When they came upon a section of more modern works, Danielle paused in front of an abstract wooden sculpture of a man and a woman, their arms and bodies intertwined. Jace had turned away to study something else, and she took the opportunity to stroke her fingers over the smooth wood.

The sculpture represented her little-girl dreams wound together with fantasies only big girls envisioned. It was a poignant symbol of what she hoped to build with Jace someday.

"Do you like it?"

His voice sounded close to her ear, his breath tickling her skin as he settled his hands on her shoulders.

"It's beautiful. It speaks of love and a lifetime of devotion." She winced as soon as she spoke. Her words hadn't been intended as a hint. But maybe her heart had chosen to speak for a reason.

He stood silently for several heartbeats, then motioned to the clerk.

Before she could protest, the study of love was boxed and paid for. A twinge of doubt tweaked her conscience. Could she and Jace ever manage a lifetime? He'd sworn that he didn't believe in divorce. But when the thrill of the chase wore off, would he change his mind? Once he'd possessed her again, would he realize memory didn't match up to reality? Without love to bind them through the hard times, could they truly remain together?

Her fingers caught the locket at her neck, looking for the reassurance it always gave her. Her father's love had been the only constant in her life until now. At times, his love had bordered on smothering, but she had always known he simply wanted what was best for her. And no matter what, since she was five, he had always been there for her, always supported her.

But she was a little disturbed to realize that she hadn't thought of him, or of the family business, since they'd left Jace's ranch yesterday. She'd been too wrapped up in herself, her rediscovery of Jace—and the possibilities he represented.

She tried to ignore the twinge of guilt.

Her father deserved to know what was happening. He was probably worried sick about the loan that was due tomorrow. But there was no way she could assure him that she'd taken care of everything.

He would know soon enough. When she arrived in his office, money in hand, he would share in the triumph. Only after they had celebrated would she tell him of her marriage.

Jace made arrangements for the package to be delivered to their room, then steered her back out into the lobby.

They wandered around the rustic expanse, reading information about skiing, dogsledding, sleigh rides and every other imaginable winter sport. Danielle wondered what it would be like were this a real honeymoon, one where they spent a week or more simply being together instead of rushing through a quick two-day whirlwind.

"Let's sit, talk awhile."

An unnamed emotion skittered down her spine. So far, conversation had only brought on arguments. Settling next to him in front of the wall of windows, she contemplated the winter scene in front of her, absorbed in her own thoughts. Jace pulled her close, tucking her against his side, then stared out the window.

She shifted, becoming uncomfortable with the growing silence, and he finally spoke. "What are your dreams?"

So different from anything she'd expected, the question threw her off balance. "My dreams?"

He twisted to face her with a frown. "What do you want to do, to be? Where do you want your life to go?"

She returned his frown, his question sparking her rebellion. "I thought you had that all mapped out, Jace. From what I've seen so far this week, you make the plans and I'm supposed to follow along." She hated to disrupt the camaraderie they'd shared, but he'd brought up a touchy subject.

He was silent for a moment. "I never intended to dictate your entire life. I'm sorry if I gave that impression."

She stared at the man who had suddenly become a stranger. Jace Farrell was apologizing to her again. Danielle didn't think she'd be able to speak if there were a fire licking at her toes.

Finally, the words to describe her dreams bubbled up, needing to be said. "I want to have kids, but we've already discussed that. I want work, to have an important place in the world, but I don't want to be away from any children we have when they're small."

She paused, hoping he would settle for her small offering, that he wouldn't force her to dig deeper into her confusion. But he simply waited patiently.

"I guess you could say I want the best of both worlds, working woman and mother, without sacrificing any part of either one."

He hesitated, seeming to choose his words carefully. "Could you be happy staying at the ranch all the time?"

After giving her heart and soul to her job for so many years, the idea held a certain appeal. It would be glorious to wake every morning without having to be somewhere by a specific time. To give up nylons and heels would be the ultimate luxury. "If there were more for me to do than cook and clean, I might."

"I could use the help. The ranch has grown to the point where I'm having difficulty doing it all myself."

Her heart sang. He was offering to share his life with her, offering her the chance to work at his side like a true wife. Still, she answered cautiously. "It's something I would like to try."

"What about *Daddy?*" A touch of bitterness edged Jace's voice.

"What about him?"

"Aren't you planning on going to work for him now that you're back in Jackson?"

She bit her lip, not wanting to dig into the old emotions just now. But Jace was forcing her to face her future, to confront what was happening around her even though she wasn't yet willing to recognize anything as fact.

"After you..." She swallowed, feeling as if she were tiptoeing through a minefield. "After we... weren't together anymore, I wanted to work with him. But he said I didn't have the education. So I went to college, got a degree in business."

She stared out the window, trying to draw strength from the mountains, needing to ignore the old hurts that were welling up inside her. "Then when I graduated, he said I didn't have enough experience. I took a job in Denver and I've been trying to gain that experience ever since.

"He hasn't let me near the business once. I've finally realized that my father believes a woman's place is in the home, and he won't back down, not even for me."

Jace's only acknowledgment of her words was a tightening of his jaw. The joy of the day faded a little for her, leaving her open once again to doubt her decision to marry Jace.

Reaching out, Jace smoothed a finger over her cheek. "I think you belong wherever your heart leads you. I'll bet *Daddy* would be surprised to know that you can do anything you set your mind to."

She blinked, trying to reconcile the support he was offering with the hard-edged cowboy she knew he was.

He stood abruptly and held a hand out to her.

"Let's go see if there's any sign of that minister yet."

Wrapping his fingers around hers, he offered a silent reassurance that he would stand behind her in anything she tackled. And Danielle couldn't help but wonder what changes would take place in her life after the wedding.

The possibilities were endless.

It was closer to four o'clock before the wedding actually took place.

Jace left her just long enough to check at the front desk. When he walked back to her, a suppressed excitement hummed around him. Danielle knew the time had come for her to pledge her life to him. Fear mingled with longing; doubt tangled with desire. And she knew no other choice lay before her. She was destined to be Jace's bride.

"It's time for you to get dressed." He smoothed a stray curl away from her cheek and she clung to the warmth of his touch. "I have a few things to look after, then I'll come upstairs to escort you."

Her stomach fluttered with anticipation.

She had just finished fluffing her hair when his knock sounded. Feeling overwhelmed with a sudden shyness, she opened the door.

He still wore the same charcoal-gray suit, but something had changed. She felt pulled, like he was forbidden fruit, and suddenly, she didn't want to resist any longer. Raising her hand, she held it toward him, urging him with her look to take it.

And he did.

Need shot through her, pooling low in her stomach. All traces of shyness fled. It was her turn to tease and tantalize, to make him ache with the wanting.

She tugged him closer. "I was having a little trouble with my zipper. Can you help?" With a smile designed to tempt, she turned and lifted her hair out of the way. It was a small tease, but the sound of Jace's indrawn breath brought her a sense of satisfaction. Two could play this game.

After all her running, she was ready to stop. And if she had her way, she would become the hunter. It had taken her all day to reach the conclusion that their physical relationship was inevitable and that she might as well enjoy it. That first time, what they'd shared could only be called magic, an explosion of feeling that had haunted her every night since.

A shiver raced over her as Jace's fingers tickled the skin of her upper back. Just before the zipper ended its journey to the top, he pressed a kiss to the skin at her nape. When his tongue darted out for a quick taste of the same spot, she felt the shock all the way to her toes.

She turned in his arms, placing her hands on his shoulders. "I believe we have a wedding to attend?"

He sighed and leaned his forehead against hers, his deep blue eyes just inches away from hers. The heat from his look singed her.

"I don't suppose we could just pretend we said the vows and get right to the honeymoon?" His rueful grin made the words a joke, but she was tempted to agree to his suggestion.

"We'd better not. The minister is waiting."

They entered the small room and Danielle was

struck with wonder once again. Just as they stepped inside, the sun broke from the shadows of the clouds. As if they'd been given a blessing, the room was graced with a suffused glow from the leaded glass dome in the ceiling. The hushed silence surrounding them generated a hope that they were doing the right thing, that everything would turn out for the best.

To add to her delight, arrangements of white roses decorated a small table behind the minister, their delicate fragrance speaking of love and commitment.

But when Jace handed her a bouquet of flowers to carry down the short walkway, her eyes filled with tears of joy. He'd even remembered how she loved roses—white roses—and the handful of fragrant blooms overflowed with delicate buds. She blinked rapidly, not wanting to ruin her makeup.

The ice that had encased her heart for so long cracked. Jace tucked her fingers into the crook of his elbow and started the slow walk. With each step they took drawing them closer to the minister, the crack widened.

The ceremony took on a surreal quality. Danielle struggled to absorb every word, each gesture, all the precious seconds, wanting to engrave this moment on her memory.

Jace acted as if he truly loved her.

The thought pounded through her brain, opening her to the wonder of their future. Jace curled his warm fingers around hers and she felt a flow of strength reaching out to her. They stopped as one to face the minister. With a gentle smile, the man started speaking of love and all that the bonds of matrimony stood for.

She experienced the sensation of floating above the scene. Joy filled her, and for the first time since her mother had deserted her, Danielle felt fulfilled. She was worthy of love, a conclusion it had taken her far too long to realize.

Now she just had to find a way to make her husband fall in love with her.

At the minister's instruction, Jace turned to face Danielle, taking both her hands in his. Bringing each hand up to his lips, he kissed her fingers, then gave her that slow smile that had caught at her heart from the beginning.

When Jace pulled a ring from his pocket, she couldn't swallow her gasp of delight. Antique gold and beautifully engraved, the simple band slid onto her finger as if it had been made just for her. As it nestled against her small engagement ring, Jace's husky voice intoned the words she'd longed to hear eleven years ago. "With this ring, I thee wed..."

Blinking rapidly, she struggled to concentrate on the remainder of his vows. The gesture with the ring was so unexpected, so perfect, that her throat closed with her emotions. She'd forgotten just how romantic Jace could be.

"Danielle?"

She raised her gaze to meet his and his slow smile answered her question. He'd planned this, had wanted the moment to be special in spite of everything standing between them. Her heart swelled as she searched his blue eyes.

There was warmth, there was humor, there was kindness.

But no love.

Biting her lip, she forced herself to ignore the disappointment, telling herself they could build on what was between them now.

When he picked up her right hand and pressed another ring into her grasp, the joy doubled. He had a matching ring for himself. He was willing to brand himself a married man, to advertise to the world that he was hers. Her voice a mere whisper, she haltingly repeated the words that would bind her life to his.

Suddenly, she was certain she was doing the right thing—the only thing possible.

She was marrying the man she was destined to spend the rest of her life with—for better or for worse.

# Chapter Eight

The moment he had been anticipating for what seemed an eternity had finally arrived. Danielle was his bride. And very, very soon, he would hold her, explore her body, hear her sighs of pleasure.

Jace watched as Danielle moved around the room, smoothing the bedspread, straightening her hairbrush, closing the closet door. Her movements were slow, sensual, a dance that teased his senses. The soft firelight gave her hair and skin a warm glow.

But the knowledge that she was truly his wife set him on fire.

Her wedding band caught the light, flashing an invitation before her hand swept out to tidy something else.

She was nervous.

Suddenly, Jace found himself wanting to draw out the moment a little longer. Now that he knew he could have her, he found himself in no hurry.

They had all night—and after that, the rest of their lives.

"Danielle."

She turned, waited.

"Come here."

It was only a second, but he caught her hesitation. When she stood in front of him, her eyes were wide, holding twin reflections of the fire behind him. His gut clenched when he realized just how strong her apprehension was.

He caught her hand and tugged until she relented and tumbled into his lap. With one finger, he traced her lower lip, the soft skin trembling slightly under his caress. "Don't be afraid of me."

Then she made the admission that almost stopped his heart. "I'm not. I think I'm more afraid of myself." Slowly, she laced her arms around his neck. "I want you so badly, Jace."

His breath caught in his lungs as he absorbed her words.

Then with a tug, she pulled him down so his lips met hers. The kiss was sweet, healing, offering a salvation he desperately needed.

His senses swimming from her touch, he struggled to drag himself away. When she tried to follow his mouth, he put his hands on each side of her head and held her still. Her eyelids were half-closed, her lips already looking well kissed, and bright spots of color shaded her cheeks.

"If you wanted me, why the hell did we have to wait so long?"

Her teeth tortured her bottom lip. "You left me little choice in matters that would affect the rest of my life. I'd lost control of everything—everything but when I gave myself to you."

Yes, he'd done that. He should feel guilty. But he didn't. Not when the reward was this version of Danielle, warm and willing.

Her tongue traced her lips, the look in her eyes an open invitation. "I choose tonight."

*Draw the moment out.* The words taunted him and he knew the reward would be all the sweeter for the wait. One more hard kiss, then he set her on her feet. "Then I suggest we order some dinner so we can keep our strength up."

She laughed, delight and surprise reflected in the sound. "I thought you were anxious to get to bed."

He stood, crowding her space, but she didn't back away. "Oh, I am, darlin'. Once I get you there, I don't want any complaints. By feeding you first, I'll eliminate one problem." He grinned. "When I make love to you, I want you thinking only about me and how I'm making you feel." Grabbing the room service menu, he sat in front of the fireplace and pulled her down beside him. "What are you hungry for?"

"You." She reached over and nibbled at his ear.

Jace dragged in a long breath of air, desperately trying to gain some control. When she traced his ear with her tongue, he gave up the battle. Tossing the menu aside, he captured her mouth, easing her to the floor. Their breaths mingled, their tongues collided, and their bodies touched in every way possible.

Then Danielle's stomach growled. Loudly.

Jace broke away from the temptation of her mouth, resting his forehead on her shoulder. Silent laughter vibrated beneath him and he smiled. When he broke into a deep chuckle, her laughter blended with his.

She stroked her hand down his back. "I guess you have a point. Maybe we'd better eat first."

Needing a break in the tension strung between them, he tickled her ribs, eliciting a squeal. As she rolled away from him, he watched the firelight dance over her, the shadows revealing and concealing. He could only hope room service responded quickly. They had more important matters to attend to.

When she stood, he remained on the floor, enjoying the view of shapely nylon-clad legs.

"I wish I had something more comfortable to change into." Smoothing her hand down her stomach, she molded the dress closer. Jace followed her movement with his gaze, then forced himself to look into her eyes.

Bracing both hands behind his head, he watched her through half-closed eyes. "I don't. Half the fun will be getting you out of that dress."

She knelt in front of him, hunching her shoulders forward so her neckline gaped just enough to capture his gaze, but not enough to satisfy. "Maybe if I just ate the chocolate the maid left on our pillows..."

If he didn't move now, it would happen right here, right now. And that wasn't the way he'd planned the seduction of his new bride.

Jace surged to his feet, then reached out to help her up. She stood slowly, remaining close enough that he could feel her heat. He touched a fingertip to her nose. "Hold that thought."

Her slow smile almost made him forget his determination to wait.

He cleared his throat and turned away. Food. He needed to concentrate on food. Then he could focus all his attention on her. "What are you hungry for?"

"Surprise me. I need to freshen up."

She disappeared into the bathroom. The bathroom with the oversize hot tub he had every intention of sampling later—with Danielle.

Picking two meals off the varied menu, he quickly ordered, adding a bottle of vintage wine to their meal. And chocolate for dessert.

When the meal arrived, Danielle had still not reappeared. Jace had paced over to the door several times, listening, wondering what she was up to. He couldn't hear anything and was amazed to realize that he missed her, missed her electric presence in the room, missed catching her glance, inhaling her perfume.

The idea that she'd become so important to him so quickly disturbed him. He didn't want to care too much. That would give her a power over him he wasn't willing to let her wield.

Still no Danielle.

Jace went to the bathroom door and knocked. "Dani? Dinner's here." The door opened so quickly he was certain she'd been standing right behind it. He eyed her carefully. Something was different. "Everything okay?"

"Sorry." She blew out a sharp breath. "I just needed to think."

Fear clutched at his gut. Was it possible he could still lose her? "About us?"

She bit her lip, hesitating. "I've always heard that without love, sex isn't truly satisfying. It was so good between us before." A frown marred her forehead. "What if I disappoint you?"

He wanted to prove to her right now that disappointment wasn't even a consideration. But he could see that she needed to be enticed, not lectured.

He stretched out a hand and stroked her neck. "Feel that?"

She shivered. "Yes."

"I react the same way to you. And the more we touch, the closer we get, the stronger that sensation will be."

He took her hand and led her to the table, seating her gently. Brushing her hair aside, he pressed his lips to the nape of her neck. Another shudder rippled through her. Then he traced his fingertips over the back of her neck, delighting in her reaction.

"You can't possibly think you won't respond to my touch." Leaning over, he brushed a quick kiss on her lips. "Or that I won't respond to yours."

The flush of color in her face assured him he'd made his point.

Rather than take his seat at the opposite side of the table, he pulled his chair around so he could sit cornerways from her. With a flourish, he took the covers off the food. Rich scents wafted up to greet him, adding a new dimension to his...appetite. When Danielle picked up her fork, he stopped her with a touch to her hand.

"Let me."

He lifted his fork and brought a piece of the succulent crab cake to Danielle's lips. She smiled, the doubts beginning to fade from her eyes, but she didn't open her mouth. He teased her with the fork until she finally parted her lips, delicately taking his offering.

He'd never seen anything sexier.

She returned the favor with a grilled shrimp. And since his impatience was growing in direct proportion to his need, he ate it quickly.

Their play became more foreplay than nourishment.

The wine that came with the meal only served to increase his need. Now. He needed her right now. And from the sensual glow in her eyes, he suspected she felt the same. Pulling her hand into his, he tasted each finger. Her eyes dilated; her breath shortened.

"I think the chocolate can wait. I'd rather have you for dessert."

Standing, he gave a gentle tug and she followed him. He let his gaze travel the length of her, knowing he couldn't bear to delay another minute. He needed to touch her, to hear her cries of pleasure. Pulling her into his arms, he kissed her while he edged down the zipper on her dress.

Savoring the moment, desperately needing to move forward, yet not wanting to end this exquisite anticipation, he kissed her lips, tracing the naked skin of her back with his fingertips. Nudging the dress from her shoulders with his mouth, he waited for it to slide off. But when it caught on her breasts, he smiled.

"Playing hard to get?"

With a wiggle and a shrug, she urged the dress onto the floor. "If I were playing hard to get, cowboy, you wouldn't have me at your mercy."

Unsnapping her bra, he exposed the ripe bounty underneath. Nuzzling her with his lips, he couldn't resist asking, "And are you at my mercy?"

His hands explored lower.

She melted against him. "Oh, yes."

He backed her toward the bed as he removed the remainder of her clothing. His own quickly followed. When she was bathed in nothing more than the firelight, he eased her down onto the bed. The only thing left to adorn Danielle's perfection was the locket. Taking her lips, Jace reached around her neck to unfasten it. But her hands on his wrists halted his action.

"No." She softened her refusal with a smile. "That doesn't come off."

He glared at the locket, wondering again at its significance, feeling that the golden heart was somehow standing between them. But he was too close to what he had desperately wanted to possess for so long to argue with her. Sweeping his hand over the length of her, he savored the sensation of skin against skin—hers against his.

"I want a family, Dani. I want to start one now, tonight. Is that okay?"

Her eyes wide, her breathing labored, she nodded.

He kissed her, absorbing the essence of her deep inside himself. It was time to end the torment for both of them. It was time to make her his wife in every way possible.

Poised above her, he forced himself to stop one last time. "Are you sure about this?"

Her gaze held his. "Yes."

Her soft answer brushed against his skin, setting off a shiver of expectation. "Once we have a child, I'll never let you go."

"I know."

He hesitated, giving her a chance to change her mind, then settled against her, making the final move to fulfill all his fantasies. From the depth of her gasp, he felt sure he was also fulfilling Danielle's.

The reality of touching her, being with her, was better than anything he remembered. Even his dreams couldn't compare with the ecstasy of touching her like this. Holding her tightly, he flew to incredible heights, making certain she rose with him every step of the way.

When they finally reached the top, sensation burst over him, searing and soothing. Her delighted sounds filled him as she joined him at the pinnacle. He lost all sense of time and space. There was only Danielle.

She was the entire focus of his world.

As he floated back to earth, Jace rolled away, pulling Danielle with him until she was snuggled against his side. She curled one leg over his and began tracing patterns on his chest.

Satisfaction filled Jace, washing away the years of bitterness and anger. This moment felt so right— like something the universe had carefully orchestrated. Holding her, loving her, was what he'd waited for, had struggled for. This was his destiny.

He allowed his eyes to drift shut, the sleepless

nights of the past few days suddenly overwhelming him. For once, he could truly rest. When he woke, it wouldn't be to the aching emptiness of a lonely bed. It would be to the warm vitality of his Dani girl.

A touch of metal changed his thoughts from what they had just shared to what still stood between them. The locket had slid to the side, resting on his shoulder, a cold reminder that everything was far from perfect between them. His fingers curled around the intricate gold heart. She'd worn it the first time they met. As reality intruded, the sense of satisfaction slipped away.

"Tell me about the locket." It wasn't a request, but he couldn't suppress the jealousy nipping at him. He sensed rather than saw her gentle smile, her dreamy-eyed pleasure in the moment. And the jealousy increased.

"It was a gift from my father."

Jace tensed. Daddy again. Even after sharing the sweetest lovemaking, *Daddy* still stood between them.

"I don't think I've ever seen you without it." He wanted to ask her to remove it, but deep in his heart, he knew she would refuse. This moment between them was too special to spoil with an argument, but the need to make her completely his, without interference from her father, was overpowering.

He rolled his head to the side, watching her face. The expression reflected there told him just how difficult the battle he'd chosen to fight would be.

Her smile was tender and she touched the locket, a gesture he'd seen her make a thousand times. It was almost as if she received strength from the golden heart.

"He gave it to me when I was five. My mother had just left us and I was devastated." She bit her lip and stared at the ceiling.

Jace's heart twisted as he watched her reliving the memories. He could see the little girl's pain. And he wanted to make it go away. But his own emptiness crept back. He may have won the battle, but the war was just beginning. Danielle didn't belong to him yet. And he wanted her, needed her, heart and soul. He wouldn't settle for anything less.

"I was having horrible nightmares, wouldn't leave the house. My dad says I was convinced he would disappear, too. Finally, he bought me this necklace. When he put it around my neck, he told me it was a symbol of his love and a promise that he would always be with me as long as I wore it."

She pressed her lips together, her fingers automatically going to her neck. "I haven't taken it off since." When she turned to look at him, her green eyes glowed with unshed tears. "And he's always been there for me."

The anger that ripped through Jace startled him. He knew Simmons wasn't the paragon Danielle thought him to be. Jace knew that Simmons was manipulative, controlling—and the man who'd coldly destroyed their young love so many years ago. *Daddy* was more interested in having the perfect daughter to flaunt in society than he was in having Danielle happy.

Burying his anger deep in a dark corner of his soul, he pulled Danielle over until she lay on top of him. Brushing her hair back, he tilted her face and held it so she was forced to look at him.

The locket swung between them, taunting him with its power.

"I've promised to take care of you now, Danielle. I spoke those vows in front of God and I take my vows very seriously."

He could see the confusion in her eyes. Absently, she stroked his cheek, but didn't respond.

"From now on, it's my place to provide for you in every way. We'll have a good life." He hesitated, knowing that his request might well dictate whether they went on to have a real marriage or simply lived together in the same house.

Fear almost stopped him. Now that he'd touched her again, he knew he couldn't lose her. But he wasn't certain he was capable of sharing her with her father, either. He wanted more than just sex and a housemate. He wanted all of her. Forgiveness for her lack of faith eleven years ago was still a long way off, but he was confident they could overcome even that.

What they couldn't overcome was further interference from *Daddy*.

"I'd like for you to take the necklace off."

She pulled back slightly, but he held her close. "No, Jace."

His heart sank. He was losing to Simmons again. The little piece of Jace's heart that had edged open, hoping to find some peace with Danielle, sealed shut again, tightly. "You're going to let him come between us—a second time?"

Her lips tightened. "I can't believe what you say

about him. He's my father. And he's always taken care of me.''

This wasn't like the past. It was much worse. Because this time, they were married, had made a commitment Jace refused to break. He wouldn't let her walk away without a hell of a fight. "How can you believe—"

She pressed her fingers against his lips. "Please, Jace. I'm begging you. Not now. Don't ruin this night for me, for us. Let it lie.''

He struggled, needing to change her mind, needing her unlimited faith and trust. Needing all of her.

But she was right. This wasn't the time. He'd worked so hard to make this night special for her. He didn't want the memories tainted by an argument.

She'd married him for the money she had to have to save her father. That had been clear from the first. Her love for her father still reigned paramount. Jace could only hope that someday he stood a chance of earning that same strong sense of loyalty from his wife.

"This isn't over, Danielle.''

Her silence was more answer than he needed.

She rested her head on his shoulder, her hair splayed out across his chest. Her breathing slowed, her muscles relaxed. He held her close, feeling her heart beat against his as he wondered about their future.

Jace watched the play of firelight on the ceiling for a long time. In his headlong bid to possess Danielle, he'd created his own little corner of hell. He'd created a life where he had the woman he wanted, couldn't keep from touching her, from making love to her, yet he could never allow himself to fall in love with her.

Because she still held the power to destroy him.

Desperate to make her his, to make her understand, he woke her with caresses and kisses, making love to her again. This time, their coming together wasn't a bittersweet, gentle bonding. He possessed her body, demanded her response and made certain she again reached the heights with him.

But through it all, the anger burned deep inside, driving him to discover a way to defeat Tyrone Simmons.

Afterward, when they lay in each other's arms, sated and exhausted, he knew he still hadn't managed to erase the specter of *Daddy* standing between them.

The sense of betrayal, the old anger, burned hotter.

She was his. He wouldn't lose her a second time.

The silence of the room surrounded them and he moved against her before pulling her closer still to his warmth.

Danielle lay spooned against Jace, her eyes open wide as she stared at the fading flames in the fireplace. The false peace she'd surrounded herself with the past two days had disappeared.

*She could love him again.*

If she wasn't very, very careful, her heart would fall for him. He said all the right words, made all the right gestures. Any other woman would be delighted to call him husband and not think about a small issue like love.

But Danielle was intimately acquainted with that cold, empty corner of her heart, a place that demanded to be filled. Without realizing what he was doing, Jace was trying very hard to fill that place and she couldn't allow him to.

In spite of everything, he'd never said the words that would let her yield her last line of defense. He'd never said he loved her. She needed the words, needed the reassurance. Without them, this was merely a business arrangement.

Over the past few days, she'd developed a new respect for the hard-edged cowboy lying next to her—enough that living with him for the rest of her life would prove to be no hardship. Especially if every night was even close to what tonight had been.

Whoever said sex without love was lacking had been wrong.

But in sharing her body with him, she'd exposed herself to a level of pain that only Jace was capable of inflicting. If he changed his mind, decided marriage to her didn't fit in with his plans anymore, she would be devastated.

Her hand inched over her stomach. And if there were a child, he would fight her for that, too—a battle that would be long and vengeful.

She'd taken a horrible risk in marrying him. Now that the sensual fog he'd woven around her had worn off, she was beginning to see just how big the risk had been. Her fingers crept to her neck, traced the chain and finally found the locket, where it rested between their bodies.

At least she still had her father. At least she knew that once he got over his anger, he would be there to pick up the pieces if this marriage went horribly wrong.

Jace's hand started a lazy exploration, settling on her breast. Warmth flowed through her body and she knew it was already too late. Whatever happened now, she would find a way to survive, to pick up the pieces and get on with her life. After all, that's what she'd done before. It had worked in the past and she'd make certain it would work again.

A low moan sounded next to her ear, then Jace was kissing her, tempting her. She turned in his arms and returned his kisses, knowing she couldn't withhold herself any longer. He had wedged his way into her life and touched her heart.

As his heat burned her, she could only hope she survived the flames.

# Chapter Nine

Danielle opened the door to the kitchen and stepped into Jace's house. Her house.

*Home.*

Strange, but it didn't feel like home.

Until she turned and saw Jace carrying their luggage into the kitchen. With a trace of panic, she realized that from this day forward, her home would be anywhere Jace was.

She followed him up the stairs, lost in her new discovery, turning each thought and feeling around and around as if she was examining an unusual rock. It wasn't until he stopped and set the suitcases down that she paid any attention to where they were.

The master bedroom. *His* bedroom.

A chill raced over her, a lethal combination of excitement and fear. She had intertwined her life with his, irrevocably, forever. Tonight, they would share this bed, and every night from now on she would sleep in his arms.

She hoped.

Jace had been very quiet on the trip home. As they drew closer to the ranch, she could almost feel him withdraw from her. The laughing, teasing man she'd spent the night with seemed to have disappeared.

His words interrupted her musings. "Which side of the bed do you sleep on?"

"I always sleep in the middle."

A grin flashed across his face, her playmate from the night before appearing for a brief second. "So do I. Should make for a cozy night."

He set the suitcases down and turned to leave, his mask slipped back into place. "I'll get that check for you. I'm sure *Daddy* is getting anxious." The teasing warmth in his voice had disappeared, leaving behind a cold caricature.

The check.

She'd almost managed to forget. Their marriage—and their happiness—was based on money, money Jace would pay for the privilege of having her as his wife.

The doubts came then. Everything she'd been hiding from herself since she arrived at the ranch Monday night flooded through her. She'd made a horrible mistake. A marriage based on anything other than love had very little chance of survival.

She glanced at the suitcases, wondering if it was possible for the two of them to move forward and forget about their shared past. Shaking off her doubts, she turned to follow Jace to his office. Once she tended to business, she could sort through the tangle she'd made of her life and her marriage.

Stepping quietly into the masculine room, she waited, her hands clenched in front of her. The scratching of the pen filled the quiet between them. When Jace finished his signature with a flourish, he looked up. Trapping her gaze with his blue-eyed stare, he tore the check from the book and held it out, not making any effort to meet her halfway.

Danielle debated about refusing the money, but the desperate look in her father's eyes that last time she'd seen him impelled her forward. She halted at the edge of the desk, wanting something from Jace besides cold silence. When she finally gave in and reached for the check, she got her response, but it wasn't what she'd been looking for.

"Bought and paid for."

The words crashed over her, ripping away her composure. Hands trembling with reaction, she took an involuntary step back. Barely able to draw breath, she forced the words beyond the lump in her throat. "I guess I'd better start into town. Daddy will be waiting."

"Danielle."

She paused in her hasty retreat, but she didn't turn around.

He softened for a moment. "Would you like me to come with you?"

Fighting the tears, she shook her head.

His grim silence accompanied her all the way to the city limits of Jackson.

It couldn't have been easy for Jace to pay out that money. She knew he disliked her father, knew the two men had always found it difficult to be in the same room, let alone get along. They were both strong, powerful men, men who were used to having their own way in the world. But those thoughts didn't make Jace's anger any easier to deal with. And it didn't make her next task easier to face.

Certain her father would not accept the check once he saw the signature on it, Danielle stopped at the bank and deposited the funds in the business account. Knowing she was in for an unpleasant encounter, she crossed the street and entered her father's office building.

When the secretary looked up, Danielle knew she was in trouble. The efficient woman, who had worked for Danielle's father for twenty years, snatched up the phone and uttered a soft warning.

Danielle smiled, but her lips trembled at the edges. "Hello, Martha. Is Daddy busy?"

"He'll see you right away, Danielle." The older woman flashed a look of sympathetic support, then politely turned away to work.

Danielle smoothed her hands over her new wool slacks, approaching the double doors as if they would reach out and bite her. But they were snatched open before she could turn the knob.

"Danielle, where the hell have you been?"

Danielle pushed past him and entered the pretentious room, waiting for him to close the door. They didn't need to wash their dirty linen for the entire company. Rumors spread fast enough in the corporate world. "Hello, Daddy. How are you?"

"My *daughter* leaves a message that the money I need to pay off a major loan is taken care of and disappears for three days. Oh, I'm fine. Just fine." His words ended in a roar.

She trembled inside but refused to let him see it. Bracing herself against his desk, she crossed her arms and watched him pace the floor.

"You couldn't have called, let me know what was going on?" He turned to glare at her. "I've spent the past three days trying to raise the money myself, but I've barely pulled in half. Your darling Raymond put out the word that I was a bad risk."

At the mention of her former fiancé, Danielle squeezed her eyes closed. "He's not my darling." What a mess. Surely it wasn't possible for things to deteriorate any further. But determined to win his attention, she squared her shoulders.

"The money you need is in the bank."

Tyrone Simmons's shoulders became less rigid, but he still eyed her suspiciously. "And just where did you find that kind of money?"

"I got married, just as we planned." If only she could leave now, without saying more, she might escape, her relationship to her father intact. For once, she wasn't going to be able to cajole him to her way of thinking. The anger in him was too hard, too controlled.

He stiffened. "To whom?"

The question echoed between them. She swallowed, praying for courage, then blurted out, "Jace Farrell."

The color drained from his face as he stared at her. "I hate that man for what he did to this family. How could you?"

She moved toward him, putting out a hand to touch him, but he jerked away. Slowly, she let her hand drop to her side, too numb to feel. Her father had been all she'd had for too many years. Now she was losing him, too.

She couldn't tell her father the truth, couldn't reveal that Jace had all but forced her into marriage. It would only make her father's anger burn hotter and he would hate Jace even more.

Danielle somehow managed a casual shrug. "It's simply an arranged marriage. What does it matter who the man is as long as he has money?" Her words sounded callous and calculated, even to her ears. But it was the only thing she could think of that might placate her father.

Her father, her rock, the one man who'd loved her unconditionally since she was five years old, simply glared at her, while the silence stretched taut between them. Finally, he raised an arm and pointed to the door. "Out. Get out of my life. I don't have a daughter any longer."

His words sliced through her, leaving her emotionally raw and bleeding. "But, Daddy—"

"You've betrayed me. I can't forgive your going behind my back and marrying a man you know I detest. No matter how noble your reasons." He turned to stare out the window, his back rigid. "Goodbye, Danielle."

Her hand automatically went to the necklace, but this time, it didn't offer her comfort. Instead, the gold heart seemed to taunt her, repeating her father's hurtful words over and over.

Biting her lip to keep from arguing further, she hurried from the room. Without saying goodbye to Martha and unwilling to wait for the elevator, Danielle hit the door for the stairway at a run and rushed headlong down five flights of stairs.

Gasping for breath when she finally burst out onto the sidewalk, she desperately searched for her car keys, her trembling hands barely able to insert the key in the lock. Just as the door opened, she heard a shout. Her father was hurrying toward her. She couldn't talk to him now. The pain was too fresh, too strong. Panicked, she jumped into the car, locking her doors before she blazed a trail out of town.

A trail that led straight to the only other home she had ever known—to Jace Farrell.

Her father, the one constant in her life, had turned away from her. The hole in her heart she'd been trying to fill since she was five yawned wider, seeming to pervade her entire being as the pain of her loss became almost unbearable.

When she pulled to a stop in the snow-covered yard, Jace walked out onto the porch. His hat low over his eyes, she couldn't read anything in his expression or his demeanor. But she desperately needed him to be the warm, understanding mate she'd shared her honeymoon with.

Stepping over a newly formed mud puddle, she managed to avoid it, then almost slipped on a patch of ice.

"Need help?" The words washed over her, offering a sense of comfort, a feel of the familiar.

"No, thank you." But he reached out anyway, offering his hand in support. As soon as his warm fingers curled around hers, the dam of emotion broke loose. With a wrenching sob, she rushed up the steps and threw herself into his arms. The slight hesitation before he wrapped her in his strong embrace made her cry harder.

It didn't matter. Nothing mattered. Except for the fact that she was in his arms, safe for a few precious minutes.

Scooping her up, he carried her into the house. As she sobbed out her agony, she was barely aware of him sitting on the couch and cradling her close. She cried for the lost little girl who had grown up into a lost woman. She cried for all the years she'd missed with Jace to hold her. But most of all, she cried for the love she'd been seeking all her life, a love that seemed to be denied her at every turn.

When the emotional storm passed, she lay with her head snuggled against his hard chest, little hiccups interrupting her breathing. Through it all, he had stroked her hair with a slow, steady caress. That rhythm continued. She savored his touch, tried to absorb it and store the sensation for later.

Finally, he broke the silence. "Care to tell me about it?"

Three words easily summed up the end of her relationship with her father. "Daddy wasn't pleased."

Jace stiffened beneath her but didn't comment.

Danielle lifted her gaze to meet his, seeing banked anger burning in his eyes. "Oh, Jace, I think I made a terrible mistake."

The anger flared brighter. "So marrying me was a mistake?"

The realization burst through her without warning, filling that empty hole in her heart totally and completely. She loved this man—loved him with all her heart and soul.

Staring at him, she let the warmth fill her like a stream of soothing water, splashing against the edges of her loneliness and washing away the emptiness. Marrying him had been the best thing she'd ever done.

"Never." Pulling his head down, she kissed him, trying to telegraph her newly discovered feelings with her lips, the words too new, too fresh, to say aloud.

He kissed her back, but there was no warmth, no passion. Desperate, she traced his lips with her tongue, urging him to open to her, to share. Suddenly, a moan seemed to be ripped from deep inside him and he opened his mouth, taking her offering and returning it with burning heat.

She broke away, needing to speak before the desire exploded around them. "Let's start over, Jace. Let's pretend that we married for all the right reasons." In her zeal to convince him, she grabbed the front of his shirt. "Let's make this marriage a real one."

He pulled a ragged breath into his lungs. "I'm sorry for this morning."

The love bloomed brighter. "I know it was hard for you. I'm sorry I had to ask for the money."

"I couldn't stand the thought of buying the woman I wanted to spend my life with. It made me say things I didn't mean."

She touched one finger to his lips. "I know. Let's put it in the past where it belongs."

He moved to slide her off his legs, but she clung to him, for once determined to fight for what she wanted. He simply twisted in her grasp until he had her pinned beneath him on the leather couch. His mouth swooped down to capture hers and he agreed to her terms without another word being spoken.

Without protest, she fell into a warm pool of desire along with him.

His hands gentle, he soothed and stroked, smoothing away her grief. She knew the pain would return later, but for now, the release was what she needed. His tender caresses turned demanding and she responded willingly, wanting to say in words what she only dared show with her touch.

Edging her sweater upward, he teased a path across her stomach. Danielle shivered as cool air and warm fingers chased over her skin. Slowly, he circled higher, building the anticipation until she was almost begging him to touch her breast. Finally, he pushed aside the scrap of lace that was the only remaining barrier between them.

The mood was shattered by the shrill ring of the telephone. Jace pulled his mouth from hers and groaned. "Talk about rotten timing." He pressed a quick kiss on her lips. "Sorry, darlin', I'm expecting a call I can't ignore."

She lay there, trying to gather her scattered emotions. She loved Jace Farrell. And somehow she was going to find a way to make a life with him. They would be happy—she would make certain of it. Now that she'd found the love she'd searched for most of her life, she would never let him go.

Jace reappeared in her line of vision, a frown marking his face. "Woman, you make it difficult to leave."

With a start, she realized that her sweater was still pushed up, temptation exposed to his view. When she saw the heat building in his eyes again, she couldn't resist teasing him. Stretching her arms above her head, she pulled her body taut and took great satisfaction in the sound of his sharply in-drawn breath.

"You'll pay for that tonight." He jerked her sweater into place. "I have to run into town for a few hours. I'll be back." His words were a sweet threat.

Danielle listened to his footsteps recede, heard his pickup start. Only then did she slowly slide from the couch. Holding her hands over her mouth, she tried to hold back her slow smile. But it broke through, along with her chuckle of delight.

Jace Farrell was in for one hell of a ride. She would win him over. He would love her again.

Realizing their bags were still packed, she went to *their* bedroom and began sorting through the clothing she'd bought. After everything was put away, she opened the box that held the sculpture, the talisman for their future.

Pulling away the packing materials, she eased it out, lowering it reverently to the dresser. She cleared a space for it in the center of the massive piece of furniture, then let her hand lovingly slide over the wood.

Two lovers, intertwined for life. It was a symbol of what their marriage could, *would,* become.

A loud knock sounded on the kitchen door, then she heard it open. Her father's voice bellowed her name and she hurried to the stairs.

"Be right there, Daddy." Hope hovered over her as she raced down the stairs. If she could repair the damaged relationship with her father, her life would be close to perfect. But when she rounded the cor-ner, she froze in midstep.

Her father was a changed man.

Rather than looking robust and confident, he seemed to have shriveled. His face was pale and drawn, his eyes empty of the sparkle she'd always seen there.

Guilt clawed at her. She'd done this. By marrying Jace. But in spite of the evidence, she couldn't convince herself she'd done anything wrong.

"Daddy?"

"Can you forgive an old man his temper?" He held out his arms, begging her for forgiveness.

Danielle didn't hesitate. She rushed into his warm embrace, her heart filling with joy when she realized she hadn't lost him.

She pulled away. "Let me make some coffee and then we can talk." She was eager to play hostess in her new home.

But he shook his head. "My blood pressure won't allow me to have caffeine anymore."

He sighed and Danielle felt the guilt grow. This was the only man who had ever loved her simply for being who she was. She took his arm and led him into the family room. "Sit down. Let's talk."

He squirmed on the leather seat and she almost smiled. Tyrone Simmons had never found it easy to apologize. Usually, she would simply forgive, but this time, she needed to hear the words. Only his saying them would start to heal the wound he'd left on her heart with his thoughtless rejection.

His gaze traced her necklace. "I'm glad to see you still wear our necklace. I was afraid Farrell would make you take it off."

She clutched at the golden chain, unwilling to admit how close she'd been to doing just that. But it wouldn't have been for Jace. It would have been because she thought she'd lost her father's love.

"Honey." Tyrone took her hand in his. "There are things here you don't understand."

She squeezed his fingers. "Then tell me, Daddy. Help me understand. I really want to."

He cleared his throat and surveyed the room. "My doctors have been advising me to retire for the past six months."

Her skin grew cold as the blood rushed from her face. "Are you sick?" Fear clutched at her. She would never forgive herself if she'd made his condition worse by her actions.

"Not sick, just worn out. That's why I wanted the marriage with Raymond so badly. Yes, we needed the money, but we also needed a man to step in and take over at the helm. Raymond was ideal for the job."

Disappointment washed through her. In spite of all her hard work, he'd never considered letting her into the company. All her efforts had been for nothing. She dropped her gaze to the floor, trying not to let him see her disillusionment.

"And since I didn't have to worry about your falling in love with Raymond, I knew I wouldn't be losing my little girl."

Danielle opened her mouth to question that statement, but her father quickly went on.

"After that little fiasco at your engagement party, I started thinking."

The seesaw of emotions wasn't over yet as a brief flare of hope filled her. Maybe he would reconsider.

"You can take over the company. You have the

education, the experience, and I know you've wanted to work there for years." He nudged her chin upward with a finger. "What do you say, honey? Want to come and work for the old man?"

Her questions faded away and the joy couldn't be contained. Life couldn't be more perfect if she'd planned it. She loved her husband, had the love and support of her father once again and would be taking over a job she'd coveted for so many years. The gods were smiling on her.

Danielle threw her arms around her father's neck. "Oh, Daddy, it's perfect. I would love to work for you."

He patted her back and murmured unintelligible words, but all she felt was the warmth of his love. He was finally willing to acknowledge her abilities, to let her show him just how good she would be at the job.

"There's just one condition."

She pulled away, certain there wasn't anything he could ask that she wouldn't do. After all, he'd just handed her all her dreams on a silver platter.

"I want you to divorce Farrell."

She watched his lips form the words, heard what he said, but her brain refused to accept what she was hearing. "Divorce Jace?"

Her father stood and began to pace. "Come on, Danielle. Don't tell me you love the man. Not after what he did to you. To us." He turned to glare at her. "He used you to get at our money."

She forced her spine to stiffen. "He didn't have to marry me, didn't have to give me the money for the loan. He must care for me at least a little bit to commit his life to mine."

"Hah! He married you to get to me, to the company. He'll set out to ruin everything we have and then he'll toss you aside."

Danielle shook her head, her body numb with shock. "No," she whispered. "He wouldn't do that." Her throat was raw with unshed tears, but she couldn't let her father see just how upset she was.

He knelt in front of her and took her hand. "Honey, it's the only way to protect what we've worked so hard for. As your husband, Farrell will have the power to take over. He'll destroy the company. You don't know this family like I do. I had dealings with his father, and the son is following the same unscrupulous path."

"Jace wouldn't do that."

"It's nice that you believe in your husband, but who was always there for you? Who held you during your nightmares?" His fingers touched her locket. "Who's with you always?"

Needing to reassure her father, to reassure herself, she threw her arms around him and hugged him close. He had to let her go now, had to accept that she'd grown up and given her heart to another man. But he also had to realize that she had plenty of love left to give to him.

"I love you, Daddy. You know you'll always come first in my life." It was time to make some demands of her own. "And I would love to work for you."

"I knew you'd see things my way." Her father turned slightly, then hugged her tighter. "I knew you wouldn't turn your back on your birthright for another man."

She started to correct him, to tell him she wasn't leaving Jace, but he squeezed her so hard she couldn't draw breath.

As she pulled out of her father's arms to continue their discussion, she caught the hint of a triumphant smile on his face. The feeling of a disaster about to happen washed over her as she backed up another step, then turned slowly.

Jace was standing in the doorway, hate and anger radiating from him in a potent mixture.

Paralyzed with the force of his emotions, she barely noticed her father's solicitous pat on the shoulder, barely heard him say he'd see her at home for dinner. But as he walked into her line of vision, she saw the triumph in every step as he left the room. And she saw him stop to give Jace a measuring look.

"You lose, Farrell."

The silence in the room was broken only by her father's departure. Danielle noted the change in Jace, in the way he looked at her, and her heart broke into tiny pieces.

"I see you've made your choice."

Tension throbbed between them as Danielle struggled for the words to explain what he had just witnessed.

"I can't believe you're letting your father manipulate our relationship a second time." Jace's shoulders slumped, the light he'd seemed to reserve just for her fading from his eyes. "I can't fight him anymore. You can have your damned divorce. And keep the money. Consider it payment for the night we spent together." He turned away from her, from their love. "I hope you live happily ever after with the family corporation to warm your bed."

Each word left a gaping wound. "Jace."

He ignored her plea. "Get out of my life."

By the time she realized the full implications of what had just happened, Jace had headed for his office and slammed the door, walling her out.

Again.

She remembered the expression on her father's face, the smirk of satisfaction just before he turned away from her. Horror welled up inside her, almost choking her. Her father had known Jace was standing there, had been orchestrating the conversation so Jace would hear the worst possible words coming from her. And then her father had twisted those words to his benefit.

Pressing a trembling hand against her lips, she knew she'd been carefully manipulated. Twice.

Jace had been right. Her father had set them up before, had fabricated circumstances to make Jace appear to be a fortune hunter. And Danielle had fallen for it, had walked away from the only true love in her life.

No wonder Jace hated her and her family so much.

Danielle became aware that she was still standing in the center of the room, one hand held out in a plea to Jace. But he wasn't there. And she doubted he'd listen to her. She'd won the battle but lost the war.

As she walked by his office, the urge to pound on the door and demand he listen to her was strong. But she still had a few shreds of pride left. She wouldn't beg for his love. At some point, he should have given her the benefit of the doubt, should have loved her enough to at least question what was happening. But each time her father had interfered, Jace had given up without a fight. Maybe he wasn't the man she'd thought him to be.

Taking each stair as if her body was racked with pain, Danielle forced herself to return to the bedroom. The same room that just a few hours ago had held so much promise, so much hope for a future. She'd even dared to wonder which bedroom would make a good nursery.

She pulled her brand-new suitcase from the closet. It didn't feel right to take the clothes with her, but it would be a terrible waste to leave them behind. Slowly, methodically, she folded each piece, remembering Jace's patience, his kindness, as they'd shopped. That day had been magical.

When she came to her wedding dress, the tears started to flow. Pulling the dress into her arms, she sat on the bed and cried for what might have been between them. The day of their wedding, she'd believed it was possible for the two of them to have a good life and find a chance at happiness. But they'd lacked one vital ingredient for a good marriage.

Trust. Jace didn't trust her enough to believe she would stand by him, no matter what.

She still wanted to stand by him. Except he'd just told her he didn't want her at his side—had proven that he had little faith in her. And she wouldn't force herself on a man just to satisfy her own needs. It would be too heart-wrenching to see the hate in his eyes, to deal with his suspicions every day.

Sucking in deep gulps of air, she tried to control

her tears. Folding the dress carefully, she hoped Jace would have a change of heart, that he would come up those stairs and beg her to stay with him. All it would take would be one encouraging word and she would be his forever.

In all the times she'd been with Jace, he had never lied to her. And now that they were married and she had the money she needed, he had no reason to tell her lies. He was a millionaire several times over, so he didn't need the money. He'd never once mentioned getting revenge on her family. He'd just insisted he wanted her. And no man could make love to her the way he had and be hiding ulterior motives.

Her father had been the only person to gain anything today—or on another horrible day eleven years ago.

She had struggled since she was a teenager to make her father recognize her as something other than his little girl, but he'd always treated her as if she were still twelve. Now she could see that he didn't think she could love him as a father while she loved another man as a husband, so he had lied to her, had destroyed her chance at love, and now her life.

And Jace hadn't.

Jace had offered her love and laughter and more happiness than she'd thought possible.

Her hands shaking so hard she could barely work the clasp, she removed the locket her father had given her on her fifth birthday. The locket was a symbol that had tied them together through the years, a talisman she had never taken off.

Until today.

Staring at the slightly worn gold heart, she realized now that it didn't offer protection, but rather was a form of control.

She'd betrayed Jace again, tarnished the trust he'd placed in her. If she couldn't honor their love enough to give him all her faith, maybe she didn't deserve him. Whatever feelings might have been growing between them had been destroyed by her lack of belief in him.

Her heart aching, she crossed the room and hung the locket on the eternally intertwined hands of the two carved lovers. Maybe he would see her offering. Maybe he would understand.

She'd lost her husband, lost her father, and lost her career.

All she could do was hope that Jace would receive her message and find it in his heart to forgive her.

# Chapter Ten

He loved her.

The ache in his chest built to unbearable proportions. He hadn't thought it would be possible to overcome the bitterness of the past. But it had taken losing her again to make him realize that for all his denials, he had never stopped loving her. And he never would.

Jace stood by the window of his office, staring at the Grand Tetons in the distance, feeling as cold and barren as the rugged, snow-covered peaks. This time, their beauty failed to stir him.

He'd lost her. Again.

She'd proven that she would always believe her father first. And Jace refused to come second to any man, ever.

He heard her hesitant step as she came down the stairs. She was leaving him.

The urge was strong to go to her, to beg her to

stay. But Jace Farrell had never begged before. He wasn't about to start now.

She still didn't trust him, never would.

For a moment, he heard nothing, then the kitchen door opened and closed. Once again, he was alone, the house ringing with emptiness.

The fading evening sun flashed on the red car as it made a sharp turn in the driveway. Feeling as if he held the few remaining pieces of his heart in his hands, Jace watched the only woman he would ever love drive away.

This time, it was forever.

The house grew dark, but he didn't move from the window. He simply stared at the path her car had taken as it left the ranch. His mind was a blank, his heart leaden.

Finally, he sucked a deep breath into his lungs. Life went on. *He* would go on. Without Danielle Simmons Farrell.

Without his wife.

The papers on his desk beckoned, demanding to be dealt with, but Jace knew he would only shuffle things around. Yet he also knew he wouldn't sleep in spite of the fact that his body ached with exhaustion. He'd felt much the same the first time she'd walked out on him.

The only solution then had been work. Danielle's desertion all those years ago had made him a wealthy man. But he could see now that all his efforts were meaningless. Without Danielle's love, his life was meaningless. He'd even tried to buy her love, but that hadn't worked, either.

A bitter chuckle tore from him when he thought about the check he'd written out that morning. The amount would have bought and sold the Farrell ranch when he'd first been starting out. Now he would barely notice the loss. What he would notice was the loss of Danielle's warmth.

Unable to bear his office a minute longer, Jace prowled the house. But every room he entered held memories of Danielle. In desperation, he went to the bedroom. That room held his fantasies, too many years of dreams where he held Danielle all night long. At least she hadn't yet shared the bed with him, hadn't left her scent on the pillows.

It was the one room he might be safe from her memory.

As soon as he opened the door, he knew that he'd been fooling himself. He could picture her that first night, terrified, uncertain, and so breathtakingly beautiful he could barely draw breath.

Jace scrubbed his hands over his face, knowing this was not the safe haven he sought, either. That left the barn. Maybe the horses would appreciate his company.

As he turned to go, he caught a gleam of unfamiliar light. He'd slept in this room for a long time, knew every shadow intimately. Curiosity dragged him forward as he used the pale moonlight shining through the window to guide him. When he halted in front of the dresser, his heart seemed to freeze in his chest.

*Danielle's locket.*

Inch by painful inch, his hand crept out until he finally touched the cool metal of the necklace. Curling his fingers tightly around the treasure, he jerked it, breaking the fine chain. Staring at the gold glow-ing in the moonlight, he wondered at the implications of her offering.

Even when they'd made love, the locket stood between them. For more than a decade, it had been an unwitting symbol of everything that was wrong with their relationship. She had refused to remove it on their wedding night and he knew then that her father would always come first in her life.

And now, the locket was here. And she was gone.

Danielle had removed her father's necklace, giving Jace tangible proof of her love—and her dreams.

*She loved him.*

The knowledge burst through him like the warmth of a spring day, washing away the agony of the past few hours. What they shared was worth fighting for, worth any battle. All he had to do was go get her and bring her home.

And once he got her back to the ranch, he never intended to let her go.

Fear touched the edges of his triumph. If she would have him, if she could ever forgive him for not believing in her, for not trusting enough.

Determination filled him. He would find her. If he had to spend the entire night tearing through Jackson, he would find her. And if she'd left the area, he would follow. He wasn't about to lose her again.

His pickup truck seemed as eager to reach the Jackson city limits as Jace was. First, he went by the Simmons house, remembering the comment about being home for dinner. But Danielle's car was nowhere in sight.

Jace felt his hopes climb a little higher. If she hadn't run home to Daddy, she must be waiting for her husband. Waiting for him.

Beginning with the first hotel he passed, he searched the parking lots. It took several hours before he struck pay dirt—several hours in which he analyzed and dissected every moment of their days together.

It had been magical, better than any time with Danielle he had ever fantasized. And some of his fantasies had been bordering on ecstasy.

In spite of his preoccupation with having her in his bed, he'd learned more about Danielle than he'd ever thought possible. And he'd discovered just how deeply his love for her ran. His love was something he would never escape, and if she refused him now, he would spend the rest of his life alone.

With a sense of deep relief, he found her red sports car parked at one of the more exclusive hotels in the area. Jace smiled grimly, hoping she'd charged it to her father's account. The old man deserved to receive the bill. Simmons deserved a lot more, but right now, Jace was only interested in winning back his wife.

After a short argument at the registration desk, he had the information he needed. Anticipation flowed through him, making his nerves hum with the possibilities, while dread hovered nearby. Stopping to purchase a peace offering, he impatiently waited for an elevator.

With a feeling of wry amusement, he knocked on the door of the honeymoon suite. According to the clerk, it had been the only room available on such short notice. Jace preferred to think of it as Fate holding out a helping hand for a change.

When Danielle opened the door, Jace observed the ravages of her grief, her suffering stabbing at him like a physical pain. In his arrogance, he had pushed her to the brink of collapse. Dark circles rimmed her eyes, an unnatural flush colored her cheeks, and her shoulders slumped.

When she saw who was at the door, she stiffened. "Jace." Her eyes closed briefly, shutting off his view of liquid green eyes. "What are you doing here?"

From behind his back, he produced the single white rose he'd purchased in the lobby. "We need to talk."

She stared at the flower as if it were something poisonous. He wanted to remind her he was Prince Charming rather than the wicked stepmother, but she didn't appear to be in any mood for humor.

Actually, neither was he. He just wanted to see her smile again, to see her eyes sparkle with delight instead of defeat.

After a long moment, she reached out and accepted the flower, a gesture that gave him hope. She could have slammed the door in his face.

She refused to meet his gaze. "I suppose you want to come in."

"I'd rather not talk in the hallway."

She nodded and stepped away from the door, the closest thing to an invitation he suspected he was likely to receive.

Danielle studied the rose carefully, avoiding any eye contact. She traced one soft petal with her finger. Jace experienced a wave of disappointment when he realized that she had completely closed off her thoughts and feelings from him.

He used to know what she was thinking almost before she did. For once, he couldn't read her, couldn't begin to predict how she would react. Even though she'd left the locket as a message, terror clawed at him. It was always possible he'd misinterpreted the message. This was his last chance to win her heart.

He opened his mouth to offer an apology just as she started to speak. "I realized something this afternoon."

He waited, silently encouraging her to continue, yet afraid of what she might say. If she told him now that she didn't love him, couldn't live with him again, he wasn't certain he'd have the strength to walk away.

"All these years, I thought I was a strong, independent woman." Her soft laugh held a bitter note. "I was working hard, being promoted regularly and living the life I thought I wanted." She stopped to pull a deep breath into her lungs. "Now I realize every move I made was being carefully orchestrated by my father. By dangling an empty promise in front of me, he kept me out of Wyoming and away from you."

She raised her gaze to meet his. The pain reflected in the green depths made him ache for her. He wanted to protect her from the disappointments of life, to shield her from any emotional pain. He wanted to draw her into his arms and assure her everything was going to be all right now that he knew he loved her.

"He always said that when the time was right, I

would take over as company president. But that time would never have come, would it?''

Jace shook his head, his heart breaking for her unrealized dreams.

Her voice became even softer. "My father must be a terribly lonely, insecure man. For too many years, we only had each other. I think he's afraid of losing me if I fall in love with my husband.''

Tightly controlling the urge to drag her into his arms and beg her forgiveness for his own lack of faith, Jace waited, instinctively knowing she needed to get this out of her system before they could move forward. But she seemed to have run out of words as the silence stretched between them.

He'd almost given up hope when she spoke again. "Why does my father hate you so much?''

It was Jace's turn to stiffen, to wall her off. But as soon as he realized what he was doing, he forced his muscles to relax. If he was going to convince her he was willing to offer her his trust, he had to start now.

Struggling with shadowed emotions from his childhood, a tangled mess only a deserting mother and an alcoholic father could leave behind, Jace somehow made himself speak. "He never told you the family history?''

She shook her head.

"Maybe it's better left in the past.''

"I need to know everything, Jace. Don't leave me in the dark any longer.''

Her plea held a double meaning that made him believe they stood more than an even chance. A chance he desperately wanted.

"The Farrells and the Simmonses had business

dealings at one time. Your father and my father. To put it simply, the deal went sour, but my dad managed to profit from it.'' He waited a heartbeat, not certain how she would react to his words. ''Your father didn't.''

''Oh dear.''

Jace twisted his lips in agreement, but there was no humor in his smile. ''Exactly. Your father can't stand to lose. My father ended up with the land where my—our—house now stands.'' Jace dropped his head forward, remembering those last years with his father, remembering taking care of a drunken old man who had given up all hope. ''It was probably the only thing in his life he'd ever done right.''

Jace wanted to stop now. The past had haunted him for too many nights.

''Your father admitted to me later that he thought his precious daughter was just infatuated with the poor guy from the other side of the tracks. He never believed it would develop into anything serious. When you announced our engagement, your father couldn't bear the thought of a Farrell in the family. He told me I would never amount to anything more than a drunken failure, just like my father.''

Jace swallowed the fear building in his throat. She had to hear the entire story. Only then could they start fresh. But he also ran the risk of losing her forever if she didn't believe him.

When she made no effort to halt his words, he continued. ''So your father set me up. He knew I was desperate for capital. The carrot he dangled was an offering to lend me enough money to get on my feet. He insisted he wanted to see you living in the style you were accustomed to.'' Jace glared at the ceiling, self-loathing making the next words difficult. "I bought the whole story."

After taking a calming breath, he dared to look at her, wondering at her reaction. She had given up so much in the past to please her father. Could she change her beliefs about the man who'd raised her? Could she give up her childhood dreams? An unnameable emotion brewed in her green eyes.

Danielle crossed to him. He ordered himself to stand still as she drew close. He couldn't gauge her thoughts, wasn't certain if she meant to slap him or hug him.

She raised her gaze to his. "I think Daddy wanted me to marry Raymond because he was safe. I could never fall in love with a man like that. And if I didn't love my husband, I would still be Daddy's little girl." Her mouth tightened. "It didn't seem to matter if I was happy or not."

With one finger, she traced his mouth. Hope began to blossom even though he hadn't heard the words he desperately needed her to say.

"When I left Jackson, I thought I knew what love was. I also thought I never wanted to experience it again. It hurt too badly."

He opened his mouth, wanting to stop her, to apologize for any pain he'd inadvertently caused. But she pressed a finger against his lips, halting his words.

"After spending these past few days with you, I've realized that I didn't know what love really was."

Hope shriveled and died before ever seeing the light of day.

Her smile was fleeting. "I think we were too

wrapped up in the great sex to think about anything deeper.''

''So that's all it was between us, great sex?'' The words singed his throat.

She didn't answer, causing his doubts to escalate. ''I've never reacted to a man the way I do to you.'' Frowning, she slowly raised her eyes to meet his. ''You scare me. You confuse me.'' She paused. ''I'm not sure I can live the rest of my life like that.''

Her words told him nothing. He was fed up with playing games, tired of dancing around the issue. Their future could be decided with three little words. Her reaction would tell him everything he needed to know.

''I love you, Danielle.'' He waited, every cell in his body pausing to hear her response.

Her eyes had been fixed on the buttons of his shirt, but at his words, her gaze jerked up to meet his. The tears that had been hovering on the edges of her lashes since he'd arrived spilled over, washing over her cheeks.

Her mouth opened but she couldn't force out any words. Finally, she swallowed the emotion clogging her throat. ''I've been waiting to hear you say those words for eleven years, cowboy.'' Joy burst through her, filling her so completely that the pain of her father's betrayal faded. Delighting in the feel of his hard body so close to hers, she twined her arms around his neck. ''And I love you.''

She waited, but he didn't speak, just watched her, all his love reflected in his blue eyes. She could bask in that look for the rest of her life with no effort.

"I want to be your wife. I want to raise a family with you." The next words brought pain just in the thinking, but she had to be certain. "If you'll still have me."

His arms remained at his sides and the doubts quickly crept in. He'd finally said that he loved her, but maybe it was too late. Maybe her lack of trust had ruined any chance for them to continue with their marriage.

Those doubts were swept away when he wrapped his arms around her and crushed her close. Just before his mouth covered hers, he murmured, "I love you, Dani girl. Get used to hearing it. I plan to tell you at least ten times a day. And I plan to show you, too."

His kiss was both a plea for forgiveness and a vow of eternity. Danielle met his tongue eagerly and plucked open the buttons of his shirt, anxious to touch him, to feel his skin next to hers.

He moaned against her mouth and backed her toward the bed, a place she went willingly. Slowly, reverently, he removed her clothes, driving her need for him to new heights. Their coming together was a healing of past hurts, and when he whispered of his love for her, she could only believe this would last a lifetime—a sentence she would gladly serve.

Afterward, she slept peacefully in his arms, intertwined with him for an eternity of love.

As the sun peeked over the horizon, Jace woke her with exploring kisses. Even after a night filled with an affirmation of their vows, she was eager to love him again. But when she reached for him, he pulled away.

"Up, lazybones."

She groaned. "I know you don't have to feed the cows and we have the room until noon, so what's the rush?" She tried to tuck the covers back under her chin, the chill of the room washing away the sleepy sensuality she'd been savoring.

He bent down and nipped her ear, then whispered, "I want to share the sunrise with you. I want to tell you I love you again with the mountains as our witness." He kissed and teased her lips until she was more interested in something else besides getting out of bed.

But he tugged the covers away. With a touch of disappointment, she noted that he had slipped on his blue jeans. As she stood, he held out her pink silk bathrobe, tying it at her waist. Urging her to the window, he turned her to face him, his gaze pinning hers.

The love exploded inside her again and she couldn't help but wonder if it would always be like this between them. He smiled, a slow, sexy turn of the lips that almost stopped her heart. And she knew she would still desire him this strongly on their fiftieth wedding anniversary.

"I want to say our vows again—for love this time."

Her heart melted. "I said them for love the first time."

He watched her. "So did I. I just didn't know it."

Danielle bit her bottom lip, trying to stem the tears of joy that threatened to flow.

When he slid her wedding band off her finger, he was so tender, so gentle, she ached. He held the ring up to the sun to capture the day's first light, then smiled at her, a smile that went straight to her soul and warmed the remaining cold corners of her heart.

Each movement slow and deliberate, he picked up her hand. After kissing her palm, he slowly slid the ring into place. "With this ring, I thee wed...."

Unable to wait, she kissed him, absorbing the words into her heart and deep into her soul.

She had come home, had found her destiny.

# Epilogue

"Did you call Daddy?"

Jace cuddled his newborn son closer, seemingly fascinated with the tiny fingers clutching at his hand. "Yes, Dani, I called him. He's on his way now."

Danielle watched with satisfaction, wondering how her life could be any more perfect. The baby had been born exactly nine months after the wedding. She'd always known their wedding night was the stuff magic was made of, but their baby was further proof.

"What should we name him?"

She chuckled. "I still haven't a clue. With the insanity of these past months, I've barely had time to remember my own name."

She had been busy, first moving the last of her belongings from Denver, then settling into life as a rancher's wife. When her father finally realized he wasn't going to lose her to Jace, he'd asked Danielle to take over the daily operation of the company, with no strings attached.

She'd been tempted. But that dream was no longer important. Instead, she had bigger, better dreams to pursue. Once she'd discovered she was pregnant, she hadn't wanted to work. Her job as Jace's wife and the mother of their child was far more important.

So together, she and her father had selected a new CEO, and together, they worked to turn over the daily operations of the corporation. Each day, when she came home to the ranch, Danielle was surprised to discover that she felt totally satisfied and fulfilled without the daily stress of work.

She had Jace, who was more than enough to keep her occupied and contented. A soft smile crossed her lips as she remembered some of the methods he'd used to keep her busy.

And now, she had their son. Assisting Jace with another expansion to the ranch had kept her from feeling as if she'd lost touch with the business world. Daily talks on the phone with her father had helped breach his fears of losing his daughter. And when she realized just how deep his fear ran, she'd discovered she could forgive him.

The door opened, letting in the muted sounds of the hospital and a disheveled version of her father.

"You always did have a bad sense of timing, my girl." But the words were said with a big smile and a teasing tone. The past months had softened her father and he was a much happier man. "Midnight is an ungodly hour."

"It's not my fault, it's the baby's," she retorted.

She grinned at her husband. "We could blame it all on Jace."

Her husband looked up in surprise. "How did I get dragged into this?"

"You're available."

He leaned over to taste her lips. Just before he pulled away, he murmured, "I'm always available for you, darlin'."

Her father cleared his throat, his face lightly flushed. "Let me become acquainted with my grandchild and you two lovebirds can continue without us." He held out his arms eagerly.

As Jace handed the baby over, Danielle laughed, wondering how she'd managed to stumble into such a perfect life. "We're finished, Daddy. For now." She turned to her husband of nine months again. "What should we name him? 'Hey, you' just isn't going to work."

"I was so sure it was going to be a girl. I had planned to name her after her mother."

Touched, she reached out to Jace and he immediately folded his fingers into hers. Then she extended her free hand to her father. Holding Jace's gaze, she made her proposal, not certain how it would be received. "I'd like to name the baby Tyrone, after Daddy."

Jace hesitated for a heartbeat, then smiled. "That's a great idea. Little Ty sounds like a future rancher to me."

Danielle's father puffed out his chest with an answering grin. "Little Tyrone sounds more like a future CEO, if you want my opinion."

The competition between these two men would probably never end. But it was a friendly competition now. They'd both agreed to declare a truce over the past.

Pride swelling inside her, she smiled at Jace, silently thanking him for agreeing to her peace offering. Turning to her father, she waited to see how that offering was received.

Tyrone Simmons, hard-hearted tycoon of the business world, was blinking rapidly. His voice was husky with emotion when he spoke. "I would be honored." He gulped, then pulled away from her hold. "If you don't mind, little Tyrone and I will take a stroll in the hallway." He cleared his throat. "You two need some time alone."

Danielle reached for Jace as soon as the door swished closed. She finally broke away from his kiss to stroke his face. "Thank you, my love. You've made my life richer than I ever dared dream was possible."

With another kiss, he assured her he was at her side for a lifetime. And with a wicked whisper, he promised her they would practice until they had another child to delight over.

After all, he would need more help around the ranch if their holdings continued to grow.

\* \* \* \* \*

If you enjoyed what you just read,
then we've got an offer you can't resist!

# Take 2 bestselling love stories FREE!

# Plus get a FREE surprise gift!

---

**Clip this page and mail it to Silhouette Reader Service™**

| **IN U.S.A.** | **IN CANADA** |
|---|---|
| 3010 Walden Ave. | P.O. Box 609 |
| P.O. Box 1867 | Fort Erie, Ontario |
| Buffalo, N.Y. 14240-1867 | L2A 5X3 |

**YES!** Please send me 2 free Silhouette Romance® novels and my free surprise gift. Then send me 6 brand-new novels every month, which I will receive months before they're available in stores. In the U.S.A., bill me at the bargain price of $2.90 plus 25¢ delivery per book and applicable sales tax, if any*. In Canada, bill me at the bargain price of $3.25 plus 25¢ delivery per book and applicable taxes**. That's the complete price and a savings of over 10% off the cover prices—what a great deal! I understand that accepting the 2 free books and gift places me under no obligation ever to buy any books. I can always return a shipment and cancel at any time. Even if I never buy another book from Silhouette, the 2 free books and gift are mine to keep forever. So why not take us up on our invitation. You'll be glad you did!

215 SEN CNE7
315 SEN CNE9

| Name | (PLEASE PRINT) | |
|---|---|---|
| Address | Apt.# | |
| City | State/Prov. | Zip/Postal Code |

 * Terms and prices subject to change without notice. Sales tax applicable in N.Y.
 ** Canadian residents will be charged applicable provincial taxes and GST.
   All orders subject to approval. Offer limited to one per household.
   ® are registered trademarks of Harlequin Enterprises Limited.

SROM99                                    ©1998 Harlequin Enterprises Limited